## "Did anyone ever tell you that you're the best husband in the world?"

"Not recently, but if you keep mauling me like that you might not get supper until later."

"What's for dessert?"

"You and me in front of the fire," he said quietly, returning her gaze. "Got anything on under that dress?"

"Black silk panties with red hearts. Got anything on under those black velvet pants?"

He shook his head.

She laughed.

But over dinner she sobered as she toasted her husband across the candlelit table. "We're making it, Tate," she said softly.

**Marilyn Brian** *was born in England and as a teenager moved to Canada, where she now lives. She has also traveled extensively in the United States. In addition to writing, Marilyn teaches creative writing, and says, "Although I thoroughly enjoy writing romantic fiction, I also write short stories, poetry, and other fiction."*

Dear Reader:

Spring is on its way—and so are more TO HAVE AND TO HOLD romances! We began publishing the line just six months ago, and already we've developed a dedicated and growing following, women (and even some men!) who love TO HAVE AND TO HOLD and buy all three books each month.

TO HAVE AND TO HOLD is the one romance line that's truly different. No other line presents the joys and challenges of married love. And TO HAVE AND TO HOLD offers the variety you crave—from love stories that tug at your heartstrings to those that tickle your funny bone. At the same time, you can trust all TO HAVE AND TO HOLD books to provide you with thoroughly satisfying romantic entertainment.

Your letters continue to pour in—and they're inspiring as well as helpful. All of you share our enthusiasm for the concept behind TO HAVE AND TO HOLD. Many of you also praise individual books and authors. From your letters, it's clear we've convinced you that, in TO HAVE AND TO HOLD, stories of marriage are as exciting and romantic as those of courtship. We're pleased and delighted with your response!

Warm wishes for a beautiful spring,

*Ellen Edwards*

Ellen Edwards
TO HAVE AND TO HOLD
The Berkley Publishing Group
200 Madison Avenue
New York, N.Y. 10016

## PASSION'S GLOW

# MARILYN
# BRIAN

**A SECOND CHANCE AT LOVE
BOOK**

*To Marilyn and Brian,*
*Valerie, Ellen, and Joan,*
*for helping to make*
*this book a reality.*

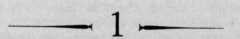

# 1

IT WAS WINTER, and the lakefront was deserted. The marina stood silent, housing only a few boats crusted with snow and ice; and the wooden docks that in summer would be crowded with fishermen and tourists now looked like two forgotten stacks of stormbattered logs.

As she stood on the beach in the January dusk and stared out at Lake Huron, Caren Bryant Ashley only briefly noted the bleakness and desolation of her surroundings. Then, suddenly, her imagination transformed the scene before her and she saw it the way her husband would paint it—an abstract symphony of pearly gray and midnight blue, of ebony and silver and pure white, these stark colors contrasting with the warm rose and flaming orange of the sunset beyond. Tate would capture the fragile beauty of the scene,

Caren thought—the lacy foam of the whitecaps hurling and splashing against the ridge of ice and black rocks at the shore, the delicate patterns of the large, fluffy snowflakes that danced over the waves.

Tate's powerful, callused hands with their blunt, square-tipped fingers were surprisingly skilled in depicting intricate detail. Those same hands were equally skilled in making love, Caren mused. Even after more than three years of marriage, Tate's lightest caress could ignite a white-hot flame of desire inside her innermost being.

As she continued to gaze at the landscape, imbuing it with the haunting lyricism that characterized all of her husband's canvases, Caren marveled at how interconnected she and Tate had become. She could share his vision, if not his talent. Not that she wanted to be a painter herself; she was proud of Caren's Crafts, the shop where she and her partner, David Halstead, sold their own and other local potters' creations to the townspeople of Russelton, Ontario, and to the tourists who flocked to the beautiful countryside. Yet Tate had influenced her work, too, Caren reflected. The wall hanging she had completed today and was bringing home to show him was her first real work of art, more decorative than functional.

Perhaps when Tate saw the wall hanging and realized the extent of his influence on her, he would start painting again. He hadn't completed a canvas since September... since she'd lost the baby he had wanted so much.

Caren shivered and tugged at the drawstrings of the hood to her caramel-colored wool jacket. Yet she knew it wasn't the cold air or falling snow that made her cheeks sting as if all the blood had drained from them. The fleece-lined hood and her thick red hair provided ample insulation against the Canadian winter; it was the painful memory of her miscarriage in the fourth month of pregnancy and the ensuing estrangement between herself and Tate that made her feel like a frozen statue.

No! Caren blinked back the tears that filmed her wide emerald eyes and tossed her head defiantly. She hadn't come here to wallow in self-pity and guilt, or to mourn the lost child she had pictured so many times. She felt sure it would have had Tate's laughing blue eyes and jet-black hair. Caren sighed and, hands deep in her pockets, moved on.

She hadn't come to mourn the disintegration of her marriage either, she reminded herself. Rather, she was here to take courage from the elements, the courage she would need to make a new beginning with Tate, to recapture the intimacy, love, and passion they'd once shared.

"I love you, Tate Ashley, and I'm going to fight to get you back," she said into the frosty air. Then, resolutely, she turned and marched back toward the parking lot where she had left her blue Mazda hatchback. She was going home to the husband she loved, wanted, and needed. She was determined to bring back the laughter and the sharing and the beating of two hearts as one in passion's glow.

Tate Ashley glanced once more at the square white wall clock as its black hands ticked past five-forty. Caren was late. Probably the snow had delayed her. Just because she had entered the house at exactly five-thirty each day for months didn't mean that anything was wrong if she was a few minutes late. She was a good driver, and having grown up across the lake in Michigan, she was used to driving in snowstorms. She could even put the car into a skid. In fact, she enjoyed it.

He recalled riding with her in the city during the first year of their marriage. At that time she'd owned a red English sports car that she drove much too fast. One day she'd taken him up a side street fresh with virgin snow and skidded till the car was broadside across the road. At first he had panicked, but then he'd spotted the mischievous glint in her green eyes.

After straightening out the car and coming to a stop, she had laughed and said, "Scared you, darling?"

"Darn right," he'd drawled, pretending to be cool. "Who showed you how to do that?"

"My uncle from Flint, Michigan. He taught me to drive."

"Well, at least I'll never have to worry about you driving in the snow," he'd said.

But now he *was* worried. It had been bad enough losing their child, but, dear Lord, if anything ever happened to Caren...

He put down the pencil he had been using in a futile attempt to translate an idea onto the canvas. Then he stared at the colorful, fanlike arrangement of acrylic paint tubes that Caren had given him for Christmas. She kept giving him paints or brushes—an incentive to work. But he wasn't painting anymore. He spent most of his time arranging the tubes in some fancy design, or reading books. He'd gone through a pile of mysteries, detective stories, and even westerns in an effort to escape his thoughts.

Lately his creative energy seemed to find its only outlet in cooking. Although he and Caren had begun their marriage by sharing the household chores, he had always been the better cook; and after the miscarriage he hadn't wanted her to top off a strenuous day at the shop by exerting herself in the kitchen. He knew how much Caren's Crafts meant to her, yet he had assumed she would take a leave of absence when, after a year of trying, she'd finally become pregnant with the baby they'd both wanted so badly. It was then, actually, that he'd taken on the lion's share of the housework. With her porcelain skin and delicate bone structure, Caren had always seemed so fragile to him. "My angel," he often whispered to her during their lovemaking; for despite her voluptuous curves, she'd always had a certain ethereal quality about her.

He couldn't understand why she had seemed to resent his protectiveness during the pregnancy, or why she had rejected his overtures at lovemaking after the miscarriage. Surely she didn't feel that he had used her sexually. He hadn't touched her once he knew she was carrying his child, and afterward he had followed the doctor's advice and waited six weeks. Perhaps she hadn't been ready then. But last month, the way she'd said, almost hysterically, "I'm not safe now, Tate," and then exploded when he'd suggested it might not be a bad idea if she did get pregnant again...

He'd only thought that a healthy, full-term baby would banish her grief. No, he admitted to himself, he hadn't been thinking solely of his wife; he very much wanted a child himself. But what about Caren? Didn't she want his baby anymore? She was always so eager to be off to that shop she ran with David Halstead.

Halstead. Was she with him now? Tate glanced at the clock; it was after six. Perhaps they...No, he

would not be a jealous, suspicious husband. Still, it
had come as a shock two weeks ago when David had
casually revealed that he and Caren had dated in the
early days of their partnership. Of course, Tate hadn't
even known Caren then, and she'd assured him later
that there had been nothing in it. But Tate couldn't
help thinking that David had been her first choice and
that *he* had only been a substitute for the man she
really wanted. Caren had been looking for a serious
relationship, and Halstead was something of a play-
boy. Then he, Tate, had come along, also seeking a
commitment... No, he hadn't been Caren's second
choice, he chided himself. They had fallen in love.
And yet—

"Stop it," he ordered himself as he strode to the
kitchen and turned down the oven. He had planned a
special dinner tonight, a duplicate of the first meal
he'd ever cooked for Caren: baked Cornish hens in
his own special orange sauce, wild rice with mushrooms, tossed salad. Even the wine he had bought in
town today was the same vintage Burgundy he had
served that night.

A lovely romantic dinner to reestablish their intimacy, he had thought. He had even gone to the florist
and arranged a colorful bouquet as a centerpiece for
the kitchen table. He had polished the silver and taken
out the good china.

Where the hell was Caren? He stalked to the telephone and called the shop, but there was no answer.
Pushing aside the curtain, he looked out of the kitchen
window and saw that the snow was falling faster now.
He said a silent prayer for his wife's safety. She meant
so much to him, despite their present alienation, and
he intended to woo her and win her all over again,

starting tonight. Stop brooding, he commanded himself. He'd better baste the hens again; she'd surely be home soon. And if she hadn't arrived in another fifteen minutes he'd call the police, the hospital...

He had just picked up the receiver when he heard the front door slam.

"Caren!" he called, relief flooding through his veins and warming him like a fine wine.

"No-o-o, it's the Snow Queen," she called cheerily.

Rushing out to the hall, he impulsively caught her up in a fierce embrace, unmindful of her bulky coat, the melting snow.

"Angel," he breathed against her ear. "I was so *worried* about you. What happened? Did the car stall? Were the roads blocked? Did—"

She stopped him with a kiss. Her lips were so cold that he automatically drew back.

"Aren't you going to warm me up?" she asked archly. "All the way home from the lake, I was thinking about kissing you, about the feel of your lips on mine. You're always so deliciously warm..." Her voice trailed off uncertainly. She had wanted to let him know that she was ready to reestablish their physical intimacy, ready to make love to him again. Why did her words sound so artificial, so stiff?

"The lake!" Tate felt his relief turn to angry astonishment. "That's where you've been all this time? Don't you have a dram of common sense, Caren? The snowstorm—"

"It wasn't a storm when I left the shop," she broke in defensively. Damn, she thought, I wanted to start off on a lighthearted note, but it's all wrong, wrong...*So make it right,* an inner voice ordered.

She shrugged off her coat and quickly hung it in the closet. "I'm sorry, Tate. I should have called."

"It's all right," he said in a conciliatory tone. Hell, the last thing he wanted to do was start a quarrel. But had she really gone to the lake in this weather?

"No, I was inconsiderate," she apologized. "And now I'm so darned cold. Tate, hug me again."

He drew her to him, planting hot, moist kisses on each of her cheeks, then seeking her lips. His questing tongue was first tentative, then urgent as she seemed to melt into him, and he reveled in the feel of the soft swell of her breasts against his chest.

A loud buzz sounded through the still house.

"What on earth?" Caren broke away, startled.

"It's only the timer. For dinner. I thought we'd have a glass of wine, talk for an hour or so, and then . . ." Inwardly, Tate groaned. The mood was broken now.

"Oh, Tate, there's something I want to show you before dinner. I left it in the car. It will just take a second."

"Never mind, Caren. I—" But Caren was already putting her coat back on. He'd better remove those hens from the oven before they dried out. With a heavy sigh, Tate returned to the kitchen.

A few minutes later, Caren entered the house a second time. Clutching the plastic bag containing the wall hanging behind her back, she rehung her coat and walked toward the kitchen, gazing around her at the house she shared with Tate. Almost the entire first floor was a studio filled with easels and benches covered with paints, bottles, brushes, and rags. Canvases were stacked backward around the cedar walls. One whole wall was a giant window with a glorious view of the bay and the little town of Russelton. The ceiling reached into a high cavern of cedar. Skylights that in daytime reflected the natural light downward were beaded with moisture from the melted snow. A small area around a gray stone fireplace was strewn with fluffy off-white rugs and bright red cushions. A stereo and speakers were set up at either side of the fireplace. The armchair she'd brought from home and covered with red velour stood nearby. She recalled her first visit to what was then Tate's house, when she'd spotted only one stool.

"Don't you have any chairs?" she had asked.

"I'm a floor person," Tate had said. "Besides, I live on a shoestring."

"Oh, I live on money," she had quipped, and they'd both laughed.

Now Tate came out of the kitchen and stood close to her. She could smell the male essence of him: the slight whiff of expensive after shave he favored, the detergent-smelling soap he used to wash his hands after working in his studio. He was wearing a tight pair of black cords and a loose gray sweat shirt that had seen better days; its stretched-out neckline emphasized the strength of his throat and his lean jaw, dark with stubble. His straight black hair was slightly ruffled and quite long, partially covering his ears and neck. He looked tough.

A delicious aroma filled her nostrils as she followed him wordlessly into the kitchen. Seeing the flowers, china, and silver, she was about to compliment Tate on his dinner preparations, but then she checked herself. She didn't want to make him feel too much the househusband or to strike a false, calculated note. The dinner would no doubt be excellent—Tate was really a gifted chef—and she would find a graceful opening for praise without seeking one in advance. For now, it would be better to show him her wall hanging and let understanding and closeness flow from that.

"This is what I wanted you to see," she said, quickly withdrawing the wool and pottery creation from the bag and holding it out to Tate. She felt a glow of pleasure as she again examined the little ceramic shell-like shapes she had fashioned with her thumb and artistically arranged among the wool and macramé. Last summer, Tate had used a shell motif in several of his paintings; and she'd deliberately chosen the yarn in autumn hues—warm brown, soft gold, and vibrant vermilion—in honor of their late October wedding. The leaves had been just those colors, and Tate had joked that it was a specially brilliant fall in celebration of their nuptials. He'd chosen the same colors for the flower arrangements in the church...

Caren's memory transported her back to their wedding day. She had been dressed in white lace, chosen because she'd wanted the best for the man she loved so much. Tate wore a navy suit that hugged his lean, muscular body, and he'd had his thick hair trimmed. Caren had loved him even more for those gestures because it was Tate's philosophy to reject most of the trappings of civilization, and suits and haircuts were two of them.

They'd exchanged gold bands in a little stone church, oblivious to the rustle of the congregation as they stared into each other's eyes and pledged their adoration. Before they left the church, when they were really married, Caren, her green eyes brimming with tears, lifted her hand to trace Tate's features—his black eyebrows, almost perfectly shaped over his long-lashed blue eyes, his straight nose, his firm mouth.

Tate did the same to her, his fingertips trembling over her pert nose and full generous mouth.

"I love you," he'd said huskily. "I love you so much."

They'd honeymooned in the United States, spending the first night in a motel near Buffalo. Caren smiled unwillingly to herself at the memory . . .

"The walls are so thin," Tate had whispered, his hot naked body covering her, his passion familiar to her but subtly different because they were married now.

Caren giggled.

"Shush, someone will hear us."

"You'll have to stuff the pillow in my mouth."

Tate had complied, and their play added excitement to their passionate lovemaking.

They had traveled through the New England states, the trees a halo of burnt oranges and reds, lakes and rivers glistening like diamonds in the crisp fall air. They'd stopped when they felt tired, eaten when they were hungry, made love when they wanted . . .

"Very nice, Caren. But I'll admire it later—our dinner is getting cold."

Tate's flat tones brought her back to the present with a painful jolt, and Caren realized she was still holding the wall hanging stiffly before her. Tate hadn't taken it, and his face was closed, his jaw tense.

He hates the shop and everything I do there, she thought bitterly. I failed to give him a child, and that's all he cares about. Maybe he only married me because he wanted a baby so much—and why does he? He never confides in me. And then there's all that tension between him and his father that he won't talk about . . .

She hasn't said a word about the meal, the table,

he thought painfully. All she can think about is my
failure as a painter. She brings her own work home
as a reproach to me, and my "domestic accomplishments" embarrass her. She questions my manhood,
just the way my father does...

Caren had vowed to fight for Tate's love, for their
marriage, she reminded herself, and here she was
ready to give up at the first rebuff. But she *wouldn't*
give up.

"Tate? I thought...Well, never mind. But I want
you to know, I love you." There! It might have been
awkward, but she'd said it. She'd expressed her feelings, though she didn't understand his attitude.

His eyes softened as he pulled out her chair for her
with a gallant flourish that reminded Caren of the first
night he'd invited her here for dinner. That dinner—
Cornish hens in orange sauce, wild rice, the Burgundy. She examined the bottle closely; it was the
same year.

"Oh, Tate, just like—"

"Caren, angel, I love you, too, so much."

They spoke simultaneously, then laughed. It was
the first genuine laughter they had shared in four
months.

As Caren unfolded the napkin in her lap, she saw
Tate staring at the wall hanging, which she'd laid on
the table.

"You've used a variation of my shell motif," he
said slowly, "and the use of our wedding colors was
deliberate, wasn't it?" His blue eyes held hers tenderly.

"Of course," she said. "And this dinner...?"

"My tribute to you—to us." With a loud pop, he

pulled the cork from the wine bottle and filled her glass, then his own.

"To us," she echoed, as they raised their glasses in a toast.

"We're like the couple in the O. Henry story. She cut off her hair and sold it to buy him a watch-chain..."

"And he sold his watch to buy her a fancy comb for her hair," Caren finished, her eyes misting with tears.

"You planned—"

"The best-laid plans—"

"Oh, Caren. I want to... I mean I..." Damn, don't make it seem as if you're panting after her, he rebuked himself. But he was. Only it was love that drove him as much as it was the magnetic pull of her body, her sensual hips, her soft, full lips.

"I understand. I feel the same way. But then your wonderful dinner will *really* get cold. And I won't be able to say I'm stuffed, and you won't be able to deliver your punchline about knowing the perfect no-calorie dessert."

"I always wondered if you thought that was a crude approach. It wasn't planned, you know."

"I thought it was the most natural thing in the world—and the most beautiful. I miss that spontaneity in our relationship now, Tate."

"Relationship?" His eyes were indigo with mock indignation. "Lady, this is no relationship; this is a marriage!"

Raising her wineglass to her lips, Caren said huskily, "To marriage, then—our marriage!" There were no words to describe her feeling of joy when he joined her in the toast.

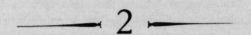

**— 2 —**

"YOU KNOW, TATE, every time you make this orange sauce, it's more delicious. What's in it, anyway?"

"You think a master chef ever reveals his secret recipes? Not on your life," he teased. "This knowledge will die with me, *madame.*"

Slyly, Caren reached for the wine bottle and refilled his glass. "Perhaps a little more Burgundy will loosen the master's tongue."

"Never," he said staunchly.

"But how am I supposed to improve my own cooking?" she teased.

"When you look at me so appealingly with those gorgeous green eyes of yours, I'm tempted to be gallant about it; but the truth is, honey, your cooking has gone from bad to worse."

"It's just that you're too damn good. Why should I bother when I can eat meals like this with no effort on my part at all?" Her voice was light with mock petulance. She felt a strange gaiety that had nothing to do with the wine. It had been so long since they'd bantered like this, and it was glorious to hear Tate's booming laughter again.

"At least you know I didn't marry you for your cooking."

"That's a comfort. But the point is, darling, you *could* be a little more generous with your superior knowledge. You *could* help me improve. Now what did you say was in the orange sauce?"

Tate shrugged. "Orange juice, lemon juice, a dash of curaçao, seasoning . . . But the secret's not in the ingredients. The fact is, I think of a certain angel as I make it—*et voilà,* the result's ambrosia."

"I'm no angel," she said in a throaty Mae West voice. "As you've surely discovered in three years of marriage, Tate Ashley," she added suggestively.

"Three years, three months," he corrected. "And for all your deviltry, I still look at you and see an angel, just as I did that first time at the lake."

"The day we met," she said softly, basking in the warmth of his gaze and remembering . . .

She had been taking her usual evening stroll along the sandy beach when she noticed a man on the shore a short distance away. She'd stopped and watched, fascinated, as he hurled small rocks into the water, making them skip neatly across the surface. He was so expert at the trick that she eventually walked over and said, "There won't be any beach left when you're finished."

Until that moment she had seen only straight black hair, broad shoulders confined within a tight black T-shirt, and long, denim-clad legs. When the man turned toward her she saw high cheekbones and a flashing white smile set in a strong jaw. But what drew her the most were the brilliant blue eyes with their long, dark lashes. His compelling gaze traversed her brief white shorts and tight white top in one easy sweep as if he were used to summing people up quickly.

"Who are you, an angel?" The soft inflection in his voice made the words sound like a caress. Caren felt a delicious fluttery sensation in the pit of her stomach.

"Maybe," she teased, wetting suddenly dry lips with the tip of her tongue. She wasn't at all put off by his bold glance. She had plenty of men friends, and she was used to their frank admiration of her long, shapely legs and full, voluptuous breasts. She had enough self-confidence to deal with even the most blatant advance.

He smiled. "No maybe about it. You're far too beautiful for a mere mortal woman."

She grinned mischievously, feeling oddly drawn to this man with the mesmeric blue eyes. "Last time I touched, I didn't disappear."

"Want me to touch?" The magical gaze was all over her body.

She drew in a sharp breath, but her glance didn't waver. "I don't usually touch on first meetings."

"Second?" he questioned.

"We could shake hands."

He laughed and scooped up another flat stone from the beach to rest it on his palm. "Do you live around here?"

"Yes."

"Born here?"

She shook her head. "I was born on the other side of the lake."

One dark eyebrow lifted. "You're American?"

"How'd'ya guess." She grinned. "My grandfather was a fisherman and we lived north of Bay City, Michigan, on Saginaw Bay. He had a summer place here in Russelton, which my father inherited. One summer, when I was five, my father came to stay and never left."

"Is that good or bad?"

"Good, I suppose. I like it."

"Obviously, since you're still here. Or is it a husband who forces you to stay, a husband and a house full of children?"

She smiled. "No, I'm single. My name's Caren Bryant. I run the craft shop, Caren's Crafts, on the lakefront."

The dark eyebrows rose again. "So you sell goodies to tourists. Gifts from Russelton. Good for you. Someone has to do it."

His sneering words were like a slap in the face. She felt her cheeks grow warm. "They're not tourist goodies. I'm a potter. I only sell high-quality, hand-crafted wares."

He seemed quite taken aback by her sudden defense of her work. "I'm sorry. I thought maybe you sold some of that plastic tourist junk. But I'm glad there's still someone around with pride in her craft. I'll have to drop in and have a look one day."

"You're most welcome," Caren told him and turned to watch his next stone skim the calm surface of the water. "You're good at that."

"At least I'm good at something," he said with a trace of bitterness.

She wasn't quite sure how to respond to that comment, so she joined him in his hunt for flat stones. At five feet five, Caren had always thought of herself as tall, but beside this good-looking stranger she felt almost petite. He must be over six feet, she thought, glancing at his long, sinewy legs. His forearms were muscled and golden, with fine black hairs.

"Here are some stones," she said, handing him her bounty.

"Thanks." He smiled, his earlier bitterness either forgotten or suppressed, although she still sensed a brooding in his manner as he gave her stones a good spin across the lake. Though not moody herself, she was intrigued by his apparent complexity.

She hung around while he hurled more rocks with amazing precision. When he sat down, she sat beside him, her legs drawn to her chin. She had the feeling he didn't want her to leave, otherwise she would. Gradually, the night eased in on them, the lights from surrounding cottages pinpointing the shore.

"Do you live around here?" she asked, breaking the silence.

"I have a house just out of town on the hill."

"Oh, which one?"

He grinned, his perfect teeth gleaming in the darkness. "Do you know every house in town?"

"Just about."

"Well, I live in the cedar one on the slope overlooking the bay."

"You do? I thought the Blakes lived there."

"They did, but you're a little behind on your gossip. They moved this spring."

She leaned her head to one side, her long red hair seeming black in the night. "What's your name?"

"Tate Ashley."

She knew the name. "The artist?" I've seen one of your shows. I was very moved by your paintings."

He shrugged. "So, I'm famous in Russelton, Ontario! How about that. I have a fan."

She grinned. "I love your work. It's . . . haunting. It sends shivers up my spine."

"Is that so?"

His eyes were an indistinguishable color in the half-light, but she could feel his gaze traveling over her full round breasts beneath the white T-shirt and then sliding over her hips and long, tanned legs. She quivered, an unusual reaction for her. But his glance reached for her and she held her breath, her chest heaving gently.

He touched her hair, his fingers opening to flutter through the silky strands while his eyes studied her features thoroughly. "If I were a portrait painter, I'd paint you."

"I've never had my portrait painted." She moved her head restlessly; his touch was disturbing, exciting.

"I should have thought the entire artists' colony of Russelton would be begging at your door."

She swallowed deeply. "No. Anyhow, I don't think I could sit still long enough."

He smiled, his hand resting on her bare shoulder. "Do you have a temper to go with that red hair and green eyes?"

"Only when I'm really aroused."

His tongue touched his bottom lip. "Oh?"

"Most of the time I'm pretty docile," she added.

His fingertip rested beneath her chin. "I bet I could get a flash out of those emerald eyes."

"Try me," she challenged, wondering for a moment where her temerity came from.

The long lashes fluttered, hiding his eyes for a second. Then he stared directly into her face. "That's an invitation I can't turn down."

As his head lowered, Caren decided she hadn't been very wise. He obviously intended to take her up on the challenge. But what had she expected? As his mouth moved exploringly, parting her lips with a soft, slow motion, it was natural to respond, to rest her hip on the sand, stretch her long legs out in front of her, and slide her fingers over his taut, muscular shoulder.

Tate's hand on her bare arm tensed and then relaxed. Huskily, he said, "Certainly very real to touch, and much better than shaking hands. Want to come up and see my paintings?"

Her fingers clutched his soft cotton T-shirt. "It's very late," she said uncertainly.

"It's Saturday night."

"Sunday's my busiest day at the shop in the summer."

"We don't have to be too long. There's a shortcut from the beach to my house."

Caren was tempted. Life in Russelton wasn't all that exciting, and it had been a long time since she'd met a really interesting man. This man interested her greatly. Her breath felt as if it were suspended above her.

His fingers drew a little pattern of circles down her bare arm. "Come on, Caren," he coaxed.

She liked the way he said her name. "Okay," she

agreed, and they parted reluctantly to jump to their feet and brush the loose sand from their clothes.

Tate slipped warm fingers around hers, and they scrambled over the beach through the darkness. He helped her across the jutting black rocks at the headland and held her waist to draw her up the cliffside to the steep pathway to his house.

She had always been curious about the old Blake place, and the interior delighted her as much as the clean modern lines of the exterior. Tate seemed to be enjoying her pleasure in his home, and she smiled warmly.

"Your eyes are flashing now," he told her.

"Really?"

"Check the mirror. Here." He pushed her toward a small mirror on the wall of his studio.

Her green eyes were wide and shining, her red hair tangled from their race across the beach. Her full lips, swollen from his kisses, pouted at her.

Tate's large hands were on her shoulders, and she saw him for the first time in bright electric light. His hard jaw needed shaving, and there was a toughness in his face that she hadn't noticed on the beach, as though he'd been fending for himself too long. She shivered, feeling an inevitability to their meeting.

"Cold?" he asked.

"No." She stared at his reflection. "You've got very blue eyes."

"Have I now? Blue and green go well with yellow, the color of sunflowers in a field or ripe lemons on a tree. We make sunshine together." His lips pressed into her hair, and his arms slid around her waist.

She held his wrists, watching their joined images

with interest. They made a pleasing picture with their summer tans, both golden, one topped with black hair, one with red, the black of his T-shirt, the pure white of her own.

"Colorful, aren't we?" he whispered. Then, dispelling the brief moment, he dropped his arms and led her through to the kitchen.

"Do you cook?" she asked, trying to shake the strange sensations she'd experienced in front of the mirror. She felt as if they'd been captured in those moments, their paths destined to merge.

"Of course I cook. One day I'll show you."

It sounded as if he meant to see her again, and a blaze of anticipation touched the pit of her stomach. Head to one side, she studied him even more thoroughly, from his gray suede sneakers up his tight faded jeans to the T-shirt that tugged at his waist, leaving a line of flat tanned stomach as it stretched over his broad chest. A floppy lock of black hair across his forehead softened his features.

Apparently amused by her blatant scrutiny, he smiled. "Do I pass?"

She swallowed, not withdrawing her emerald gaze from his dark blue one. "Oh, I think so."

His eyes lowered, and she saw his chest heave slightly. "You pass, too."

"Good." She smiled, wanting to lighten the atmosphere.

He shifted his feet. "Can I offer you a drink? Beer, coffee, tea?"

"Well..." Caren's moist palms ran over the curve of her hips in the brief white shorts. She really should get home.

"Let's have some coffee." He placed a battered stainless-steel kettle on the stove, then took out two mugs and filled them with instant coffee. The kitchen clock read eleven-forty-five.

"Where did you live before you came here?" she asked.

"I have an apartment in Toronto, but I thought if I came out here alone I might get more work done."

"Well, there's not much doing in Russelton," she said. "You picked a good place for peace and quiet."

"That's what I'd hoped," he said softly.

Her eyes met his, and she had the uncontrollable urge to move closer, to touch his high cheekbones, stroke the long black lashes. She recalled his kiss on the beach, the slow sinking sensation. "Well, don't let me bother you."

His mouth took on a vulnerability, his hard features seemed to soften. "I find you very . . . disturbing," he whispered hoarsely.

"Do you?"

A whistling sound sang through the kitchen. Suddenly he grinned. "Saved by the kettle." Moments later he was handing her a full mug of steaming coffee. "Do you take anything in it?"

She shook her head. "No thanks."

"Neither do I." He opened a pottery cookie jar and told her to help herself.

Biting into a chocolate-chip cookie, he leaned against the counter. "Where do you live?"

"Above my shop."

"Alone?"

"Yes, since my mother died."

"I'm sorry."

"She died six years ago. My dad died when I was sixteen. You see, I was born quite late in their marriage, and they weren't young."

"Were you an only child?"

"Uh-huh," she said. "What about you?"

"My parents live in London, Ontario, and I have two older brothers."

"Are they artists?"

"Hell, no! My dad very carefully cultivated a family construction business, George Ashley and Sons. The other two are part of that. I'm considered the black sheep of the family."

"What happened?" She sensed that there was much more to this story.

"I left school and home at seventeen to become an artist. That didn't go over very well with my parents, and I was under a lot of pressure to prove myself as a painter, to justify what I'd done. Now I'm beginning to wonder whether I shouldn't have gone into the construction business." .

"Why do you say that?"

Tate shrugged his broad shoulders. "For years I struggled to make it as an artist. A few years ago my paintings finally started to sell. I even began to make money. A lot of money. I got caught up in the image of it—all the publicity, you know—the image of myself as the brilliant, successful young artist. I haven't painted much since. I have the feeling that whatever I paint won't live up to what's expected of me. I spend a lot of time standing back from my work, wondering if it will sell, instead of doing it."

Caren nodded. "I understand."

He drained his coffee mug and placed it on the

counter. "So I'm hoping that moving here, putting myself in new surroundings, will get me out of that slump. I'm away from the city, away from its temptations, away from the people who demanded my time."

"I hope you succeed," she told him sincerely. "I'm not just trying to flatter you when I say I admire your work. I truly do."

He held her glance. "I believe you."

They looked at each other for a long time, and once more Caren felt the desire to move toward him, to touch him.

If she didn't get out of here soon, she just might end up in his bed. The thought of making love to Tate filled her with a sensation of warmth that confused and unnerved her. She swung around to put down her cup. "Anyhow, I thought you were going to show me your paintings before I turn into a pumpkin."

He smiled. "Of course. Come on."

He led the way back into the studio and stood in the middle of his artistic muddle. "What do you want to see first?"

"What are you working on now?"

"Nothing much. Here, I'll show you some things that were in my last show." He began turning canvases around to face her, and Caren knelt on the floor to have a close look.

"I love this one," she said. It was blue, green, and yellow, an abstract symphony of water, earth, and sun.

"You can have it," he told her. "It's a present."

"I can't accept this. It must be worth a fortune!" She was still kneeling on the hard wood floor.

"Money's not everything," he said, grinning. He leaned down to pick up the painting. "I'll wrap it for you."

"I can't believe it!" Getting to her feet, she watched as he expertly wrapped the small canvas in brown paper.

He secured the last piece of tape. "Just don't sell it at a profit and retire." He handed the painting to her.

She laughed, but her voice was strangely solemn as she told him, "I'll treasure it forever, Tate." Then she glanced at his clock. "I must go now."

"I'll walk you home."

He took her home the long way—down the winding driveway away from his house, along the gravel shoulder of the highway, down the main street past all the silent red-bricked old houses, and to the lakefront. At the door of Caren's Crafts, he leaned over her, one hand on the doorpost. "I want to see you again, Caren."

"I'd like that," she told him, as one hard thigh brushed the soft nakedness of her own and a warmth crept through her stomach.

"I hoped you'd say that." His hand brushed her luxuriant red hair from the side of her face, slipping it over her shoulder. His chest muscles flexed, and he leaned forward. She closed her eyes, waiting for his second kiss. His mouth fluttered over her lips. Then he straightened and slipped his hands into his back pockets. "I'll call you, Caren."

"Good night, Tate, and thank you."

She stood at her door, watching him walk down to the beach through the still summer night. Clutching his painting, she slipped into her silent shop and climbed the stairs to her apartment.

When she awoke the next morning, her first thought was of Tate. And even as she bent over her work, she couldn't shake him from her mind. That evening, and several evenings afterward, she wandered the beach, hoping to see him, but each time she was disappointed.

When the chimes on the shop door clanged gaily one afternoon, she looked up to greet her customer with her usual happy smile.

"Tate," she said softly, watching the man in jeans and denim shirt walk toward her.

"Caren." He grinned in reply and leaned against the wooden counter.

"I've missed you," she told him, her nostrils picking up the slight edge of after shave and soap from his skin.

"And I missed you. I was down in Toronto cleaning up the rest of my business."

"Then you really are moving here?"

"Yes, I've decided to live here."

A precious thrill ran through her body at the realization that she might see him regularly. Her fingers curled into fists. "I'm so glad."

He touched her hand, covering her delicate fingers with his large ones. There were dark hairs on his wrist, and a black watchstrap that contrasted with his golden tan. He gripped her hand. "I've more than missed you," he confessed.

"Me, too," she told him honestly, linking her fingers with his. It seemed so crazy that after only one meeting they could be so sure . . .

\* \* \*

"Caren?" Tate's voice interrupted her reverie. "I was wondering if you'd like something else. I could make some cocoa for us to drink in front of the fireplace. This morning I chopped some more wood and laid a fire on the hearth."

"Mmm, sounds lovely. I feel I should offer to make the cocoa, but somehow scorched chocolate doesn't seem like the perfect ending to this perfect meal." She flashed him a grin. Her ineptness in the kitchen was a long-standing joke between them.

But Tate had no answering grin for her. "It's not that, honey," he said seriously. "It's just that I don't want you to overexert yourself. You—"

"Tate, for goodness' sake, I'm all right!" The doctor had said she was fine now, so why did Tate act as if she were some kind of delicate machinery whose works had been mangled or damaged? Was that what she was to him now—a baby machine that had malfunctioned? He'd seemed to want that child more than he wanted her, and she had a feeling that there was something obsessive about it, something he was keeping from her.

"Caren, please, let's not quarrel. It's been so good tonight, almost the way it was . . ."

"Before I had the miscarriage," she finished flatly. "We have to talk about it, Tate. About the baby, about what's happened to us."

"Later. Let me get the fire started, make the cocoa. You just stretch out on the hearth and relax, honey."

After he had a roaring fire going, he headed back to the kitchen, leaving Caren lying on the rugs before the fireplace. They'd made love for the first time on those very rugs, he recalled. After eating the dinner he'd cooked for them—the same meal he'd tried to reproduce tonight—Caren had gone to the hearth and laid down on the rugs, staring at the empty fireplace as a summer thunderstorm raged outside.

"Why don't you build a fire?" she'd said, rolling on to her stomach, her bare tanned legs swinging back and forth.

"It's summer." He sat down beside her and stroked her back, his fingers playing with the edge of her red hair where it met the pale mauve cotton sundress. "Redheads aren't supposed to wear mauve, are they?"

She turned on her back and looked up at him. "This one does anything she wants."

"Anything?" His tongue touched his bottom lip lecherously.

"Anything," she echoed recklessly, and pulled his hand down to her breasts, which yielded beneath the soft cloth. "Touch me, Tate . . ."

Her nipples were taut and ripe, and a wild, savage desire surged through him. She excited him as no other woman ever had . . . and he loved her. Suddenly, he felt an overwhelming need to tell her what she meant to him.

"I love you, Caren. You've made this the most beautiful, contented summer of my life."

"And mine, my darling." She pulled him down to her, tangling her fingers in his straight black hair.

They lay for a long moment, silent, their hearts beating with the rhythm of the waves crashing on the rocks below.

"I never thought I'd ever be this happy," he told her.

"I've always been happy, but never *this* happy."

He lifted himself on his elbow. "You're not teasing me?"

"I'd never tease you about that," she said, her fingers fluttering over his hard jaw.

"Then tell me you love me."

"I love you, Tate."

They kissed, their lips parting, tongues tasting sweet as wine. He drew down the zipper of her dress.

"You know how to do that very well," she whispered.

"I've had all summer to practice on you." He slid the material down to her waist, arranging her hair gently around her bare shoulders. He drew her dress down her hips and tossed it into the pile of cushions. "Caren, let me love you tonight."

"Please." She nodded, her fingers eagerly reaching for the little white buttons of his denim shirt. She pushed it from his shoulders, and impatiently Tate flung it aside. Playfully, she poked his belly button. But the fun turned to a moan of harsh desire as his tongue flicked over the fullness of her breasts.

He grinned. "You're a tease." His eyes glanced down her long limbs to the little mauve bikini panties. "Look at you. You're so beautiful, so fresh. Oh, my angel..." His mouth crushed hers, and the teasing ended.

Caren arched her body into his, helping him to remove his jeans. The flimsy mauve panties flipped through the air to join the rest of the discarded garments. He inhaled her scent, heady with the intoxication of it.

Shivering with ecstasy, she slid languorously beneath his body, crying out, "Don't stop, don't ever stop."

"Never," he assured her breathlessly, shifting his hard body over hers. She was so sweetly wet, so gloriously ready.

Their bodies were perfectly attuned. He teased and tested her reactions, discovering what pleased her, as she drove him nearly beyond control. And then there was no teasing, no testing. A thunder pounding in his veins, they soared upward together.

"Tate, yes, Tate, yes," she cried and he took her where they both wanted to go, the lightning from the storm crashing around them in the hot summer night...

A violent tremor swept through Tate at the memory of their first lovemaking, and he gripped the counter to steady himself. Dammit, he wanted her so much. Didn't she feel the same frustrated desire that he felt? Or was she having an affair with David Halstead? Had she been at Halstead's apartment tonight, in his arms? She'd recently remarked that Halstead no longer seemed as confirmed a bachelor as he'd once claimed to be. Was she hoping to marry the guy herself after getting a divorce?

Tate reached into the overhead cabinet for the container of cocoa and slammed it onto the counter. She might be planning to leave him, but for the moment she was still his wife. And starting tonight they were going to have a real marriage again, in every sense of the word.

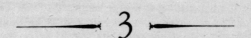

## 3

WHEN TATE CAME in with the cocoa, Caren saw at once that the brooding look was back in his eyes. She sat up and drew a small, wrought-iron table over toward the fireplace; Tate put the cocoa on the table and sat down beside her.

Abruptly, he blurted out, "Do you realize we haven't made love for six months, Caren?"

"Of course I realize it," she said defensively. "Tate, that's one of the things I want to discuss. There was no need for us to stop making love just because I was pregnant."

"I didn't want to take any risks!" It was his turn to be defensive. "But afterward, you rejected me."

"Oh, Tate, I didn't mean to *reject* you. Don't take it that way, please." Instantly, her heart softened to-

ward him as she realized the agony he must have been
going through. She'd been so caught up in her own
agony... She had to make him understand.

"How else could I take it?" he demanded, raking
a hand through his thick black hair.

She reached for one of the cocoa mugs and gave
it to him, deliberately brushing her fingers over his
in the transfer. With that brief touch she tried to con-
vey all her love for him, but his eyes were filled with
pain as he took a sip of the hot drink and waited for
her to speak.

She drank from the other mug, first, letting the
cocoa's soothing warmth relax her. "Losing the baby
was the worst thing that ever happened to me, Tate.
Worse even than when my parents died. There's something about the death of a child..."

"It wasn't a child yet."

"It was to me! Our child—our son. Perhaps learning the sex of the baby made it worse, more real. At
first I was just in shock; but after the numbness wore
off, I plunged into the worst abyss of grief and pain
I'd ever experienced.

He put his mug back on the table, then reached
over and lightly caressed her hair. "You cried so much,"
he said softly. "I'd never seen you cry before. You
were always so cheerful, like a ray of sunshine, off-
setting my own moodiness." He paused, frowning.
"If it hadn't been for me, you'd still be the vibrant,
exuberant person you were when we met. I changed
you, Caren. It was my fault."

"No!" Impulsively, she reached for his hand, holding it in hers. "We both wanted to have a child."

"But you didn't want to try again."

"Please, Tate, let me explain." She squeezed his hand gently, a plea for patience.

"All right, Caren. I'm sorry."

"You're still blaming yourself, Tate. But you see, I was in mourning for the child that died. The idea of a substitute, a replacement, was upsetting. People kept saying that to me, you know: 'You ought to have another child; that will make you forget.' But I didn't want to forget. I needed to mourn, as if somehow that could make up for all the years our son would never have. And there's more, too, Tate. I felt guilty because, much as I'd wanted to get pregnant, sometimes it seemed as if the baby was more important to you than I was, and—"

"Never!" he broke in. His eyes looked searchingly into hers, and she felt the warm pressure of his fingers in her hand. "You really thought that?"

"Yes. Tate, when we first got married and agreed to wait a year before trying to have a child, I felt you weren't completely comfortable with that decision. Part of you wanted us to have that time alone together, but part of you wanted a child right away. I saw that especially when you were with your nephew, Mark. The wistful look in your eyes... Anyway, when we did try, and I didn't get pregnant right away, you seemed very anxious, even though the doctor said it often took time. And then, when I was carrying the baby, it was almost as if I didn't exist for you anymore except as the mother of your child."

"That's absurd!" She felt his hand stiffen in hers.

"Is it? Suddenly, you kept telling me not to strain myself. You wanted me to abandon the shop and stay home and rest all day."

"I was concerned. And maybe a bit jealous of the shop. Of course, I didn't know about you and Halstead then."

"Tate, for pity's sake!" She resisted the impulse to jerk her hand away from his, but the insinuation of his words stung her to the quick. She was trembling with hurt and indignation. "How many times do I have to tell you? There was never anything between us. David and I had a few casual dates—"

"That you never mentioned to me! The first time I met him in the shop, you said only that he was your partner and a friend."

"That's all he was! I think we were both aware that the partnership wouldn't work if we got involved— unless it turned out to be the love of a lifetime. So we dated a few times, got to know each other better. The liking deepened, but that was all. I guess I realized from the start that David and I could never be more than friends. I'd always sensed that for me love would happen at first sight or not at all. And then I met you . . ."

"There's the old saying about marrying in haste and repenting at leisure," he said, probing. Her explanation of the dates with Halstead seemed logical enough, but perhaps things had changed now.

"I haven't repented of our marriage, Tate. I want to get it back on the right track again. I want us to be close, but you don't share your deepest feelings with me anymore. Like the baby. There was something almost . . . abnormal—"

"There was nothing abnormal!" he denied. The word was like a blow, recalling the terrible time his father had said, "Your brothers are what's called regular guys, Tate. But you seem to go out of your way to be abnormal."

"Tate, what is it?" He felt the pressure of her hand squeezing his, saw the concern in her eyes. Caren was only trying to understand. Maybe he should open up, tell her everything. No, he couldn't. It was painful enough just thinking about it; and he was afraid, too. If Caren knew what his father really thought of him . . .

"Caren, love," he said, "sometimes it's so hard for me to put things into words. Talking doesn't always come easily to me. I'm an action person. I use my hands—I paint, I chop wood, I cook—that's how I deal with my feelings."

"That's not dealing with them, Tate."

He sighed. "I guess I'm not ready to deal with everything at once. I'm not trying to shut you out, honey, just asking you to bear with me. Over the years, I've told you things I've never told anyone else. But we were close in other ways, too, and that made it less difficult."

"I know. I miss those other ways of communicating, too. We've made a start tonight, Tate. That's what's important." Her hand left his and traveled upward, tracing the chiseled planes of his face. When her fingertips brushed his lips, his tongue darted out and licked them.

She smiled. "Was that a kiss, or were you just trying to taste the little dab of orange sauce on my finger?"

"I know a nectar that's sweeter than orange sauce," he said huskily, drawing her close and bending his head to hers. Her lips were warm, tasting faintly of cocoa and wine, and their pressure was as urgent as his own. His questing tongue met hers as the kiss deepened, and he felt the soft swell of her breasts pressing tightly against his chest. He was conscious of his own hard arousal between them.

He traced one hand along the curve of her hip. "There didn't used to be so much bone here, angel," he remarked.

"I've lost weight," she conceded. "Feed me with love, Tate."

He wasn't sure of his control. Her mouth was open, so sweet . . . She was so soft against his granite body. He buried his warm mouth in the fullness between her breasts, his hand unfastening her bra and then pushing beneath her blouse to cover her nipple. He massaged it with his thumb in the way she liked, and she groaned into his ear, nibbling at his lobe in the way he liked.

She gasped as the pressure on her breast sent waves of desire coursing through her limbs. She'd been re-pressing her sexual needs for months, and now they burst forth with one single caress. She moved against the length of his body. "Oh, Tate . . ." She was aflame with longing and need.

"Yes, angel, yes." He almost tore the blouse off her and flung it aside. Her skirt and underthings were disposed of in the same manner. He held her to him, her nakedness against the barrier of his clothes ex-citing him no end. She was pulling at his sweat shirt, dragging it over his head. Then her naked breasts swelled against his chest, her nipples hard little buds. He lowered his mouth once more, his tongue lapping at her flesh, her satiny silky skin. His hands caressed her thighs, and she opened for him, warm and moist.

Caren's fingers shakily eased the zipper on his cord pants. She wanted him. Her body was on fire, burning dizzily with her need. It made her primitive, almost animal. She cried out at each tender, urgent touch.

He kicked off his cords and they both lay side by side on the white rug, their flesh warmed by the fire and by each other. "Caren, Caren." His heated breath trailed over her throat and breasts as he tried to hold off from taking her too quickly. He wanted this to be right and perfect, but he wasn't sure he could wait that long. She was writhing against him, and there was a sheen of sweat between them that made her slippery and sensuous. He never wanted this to end. He wanted to make love to her forever, not just tonight, now, but on and on, into eternity...

She wasn't aware of anything anymore but her need, the throbbing pulse racing through her veins, the sweaty heat of their bodies that radiated and drew them together as one. Always this closeness with Tate, this desire that drove them both mad. He moved into her at long last, and she arched for him, opening herself completely, offering every part of her body that he desired. She was able to touch him where she pleased. Her hands moved down his spine to his firm buttocks to hold him closer. She was near to fulfillment. She could feel the little sparks bursting, stretching out for him.

"Tate," she cried out. "Oh, Tate."

He was drowning in her. All he could sense was Caren and the driving pressure for release. He drew her hips up closer, harder, and he could feel her near.

Little explosive lights were going off in her head, and her body felt wired to the charge as it quivered with joy. Tate was with her all the way, calling her name.

He didn't leave her, but shifted slightly above her.

His mouth trailed hotly over her eyelids, her cheek-bones, her nose, her mouth. His tongue slipped to her ear, and he licked the lobe.

"I don't want to stop," he said huskily.

She curved into him. "Don't then. Keep going."

"Insatiable lady," he whispered.

He moved inside her, and she felt him hardening again. "Animal," she whispered back, nipping his earlobe playfully.

"You know I always have a hard time stopping." His tongue was still circling her ear.

"Did I ever tell you to stop?" she gasped as the pressure began to build inside again.

"Tell me what you want, Caren."

"A bit of this," she said, sliding her long silky legs between his hair-roughened ones. She rubbed the top of his muscular thighs with her fingers and laced them around to his inner thighs. He groaned with pleasure, and she continued her probing until he throbbed within her again.

Once more her breath was mingling urgently with Tate's, their tongues entwined, their bodies rocking in a rhythmic dance. He drew her over on top of him and she looked down into his blue, passion-filled eyes and breathed, "Oh, Tate. Why ever didn't we—"

"Never mind. We just have to make up for lost time, that's all."

She swept her long red hair across his face mischievously, and then she tensed. "Now, Tate. Now!"

He tensed with her and pleasure shot through one to the other, their bodies fused. Caren closed her eyes and let herself be drawn upward before she finally landed, feeling soft and satisfied.

Tate lay on his back and gazed tenderly at Caren

beside him, her ripe, naked body languorous. The intensity of their lovemaking made him quite sure that she hadn't been in David Halstead's bed tonight—or any other night. She was his woman, his wife; the jealous demons were laid to rest. But there were still things to be talked out. Perhaps now, while he felt so close to her, he should tell her about his father.

But he heard her gentle breathing and realized she had dozed off. He rose to his feet and tenderly scooped her sleeping form into his arms, then carried her upstairs to the bedroom. She was light and precious in his arms.

She awoke as he was trying to put a nightgown on her. "Not yet," she said drowsily, taking the garment from him and languidly tossing it to the floor. "I'm insatiable, remember? Unless you—"

"Me? I'm the original caveman," he teased with a playful leer.

She grinned as her arms entwined about his neck. "And all this time, I thought you were my husband."

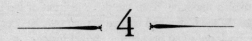

# 4

IN THE MORNING, Caren crept out of bed, took a shower, and dressed in jeans and a salmon-pink sweater. Tate was still sleeping, turned on his side, his arm wrapped protectively around his pillow. There were little green flowers on the pillowcase, and they looked very feminine against his hard, masculine arm. His skin had lost all traces of summer tan, and the dark hairs on his flesh accentuated the pallor. The lines that usually fanned out from his eyes were smoothed in sleep, and she smiled. He looked like an innocent little boy. Determined to further their truce, she knelt by the side of the bed and kissed the tip of his nose.

"I'm leaving for work now," she told him softly.

He groaned and pulled at the cover, which was

down below his waist. "Tate," she said, "I'm going to work. Wake up."

His long lashes fluttered open, and she remembered the first time she had ever seen his dark blue eyes, and how they had fascinated her. They still did.

"What time is it?" he asked thickly.

"Eight-thirty. I'm leaving in a minute. I want a good-bye kiss."

"What about the snow?"

"It's not that bad."

"I'd better shovel." He kissed her nose affectionately and swung his long legs over the bed.

Dressed in jeans and a hooded navy parka, Tate shoveled the snow from the drive in front of the garage. When Caren had backed her car out, he opened the back door and pushed the shovel inside.

"You might need it later. It looks like it's going to snow again." He leaned on her rolled-down car window. "Did you say something about a good-bye kiss?"

"I thought we should start that again," Caren said. "Don't you?"

"I certainly do." His mouth moved over hers. Their lips were cold, but the kiss was warming.

"You've got the most kissable lips in the world," he murmured.

Her tongue outlined his lower lip. "Want me to go to work or not?"

"I could find lots to do with you in the house."

"I won't be late tonight, Tate," she whispered, and gave him one extra kiss. "Save it for me."

He smiled. "You sexy temptress. Get out of here."

Caren drove the car protestingly down the winding, sloping driveway. The highway was icy, and the strong wind blew the car from side to side with such force that she had to clutch the steering wheel with all her strength. She was relieved to reach the main street.

Slowly, she drove past the red brick houses to the lakefront. Lake Huron was a furiously tossed gray. She parked beside the store and ran through the stormy gusts to the door. David lived in town and walked to work; she knew he would already be there. Stamping the snow from her boots, she took off her coat.

"I wondered if you'd make it," David said. He was mixing clay with water for the pots he planned to throw that day.

"I never contemplated not making it," she told him, peering out the window at the blowing snow. "But I am wondering about getting those pots shipped."

"Give the shipping company a call, and they'll come when they're ready." David shrugged. "What can you do in winter?"

Stay home and keep warm making love with Tate, she thought while she put the kettle on to boil for instant coffee.

She looked at David, remembering Tate's jealousy last night. She couldn't deny that David was attractive with his curly blond hair, tight faded jeans, and black turtleneck pullover, and she was aware of the tightly muscled body beneath his clothes. She had seen him in summer often enough, dressed in shorts or swim gear.

Still, there was only one tightly muscled body she responded to, and that was Tate's. She thought of their previous night's lovemaking and lit up inside like a Christmas tree. She hoped there would be a repeat performance tonight. Eventually, they might just love their problems away.

"Earth to Caren, Earth to Caren." David flicked

his head. "Your kettle's boiling."

"Thanks." Caren turned to prepare her coffee.

They both worked hard at the wheels all morning, listening carefully in case the door chimed. But of course it wouldn't. Who'd come out on a day like this to buy pottery?

When the chimes did jingle, Caren and David both looked at each other in surprise. Caren stepped into the shop to see Mrs. Stark, the owner of the local motel, examining the goods on the shelves. Grace Stark was in her late forties but still slim and attractive, even bundled into a purple ski jacket, black slacks, and matching high leather boots. Usually the Starks closed up shop and went south for some of the winter, but this year they had chosen to stay home.

"Hi, Caren." Grace Stark smiled. "I bet you didn't expect to get a customer on a day like today."

Caren returned the smile. "You're right. What can I do for you?"

"My nephew Tony is getting married. It's quite sudden, but I thought I'd give them a nice casserole or something."

Caren moved around the counter to stand beside her and pointed to a caramel-colored dish that David had made. "It comes with matching soup bowls and lids," Caren said.

"Now that looks nice. Maybe you could wrap it up for me. I thought I'd get this taken care of first, before I try and decide what to wear. I'll probably have to go into the city and look for something there."

"It's not exactly Fifth Avenue here in Russelton." Caren laughed, taking the dishes from the shelf. She wrapped them in orange tissue paper and began placing them in a glossy brown gift box.

Grace Stark watched her. "We haven't seen you or Tate at the Cross-Country Ski Club this year."

Caren's fingers clenched around the edge of a soup bowl. "We've been busy."

"Not that busy, surely. What's there to do in Russelton anyway, when the day's work is finished? You should come out to the next meet. We're planning on having an afternoon's run followed by a buffet dinner and dance. I'm sure you'll enjoy it. Remember what a good time we had last year?"

Caren nodded, her mind flashing to a small montage of that happy day: she and Tate giggling in the snow, dancing to loud rock music late into the wee hours. Despite last night's intimacy, she couldn't see them doing that this year. He was still so protective of her.

"I'm not sure," she told Grace, carefully placing the soup bowls and lids around the casserole dish in the box. "I'll talk to Tate, though."

"You do that. I'll give you a call as soon as the final arrangements have been made. You'll have to bring along a dish of food, that's all."

"Okay," Caren agreed. Maybe they should go to the meet; getting their social life back on keel might help the marriage in other ways, too. If she could convince Tate . . . "Do you want this gift wrapped?"

"No. I'll do it myself, dear. I have some silver paper and ribbons at home." Grace held the box carefully in her hands after she'd paid for it.

"Have a nice time at the wedding," Caren said. "And give our best to Tony."

"I will. See you around."

"Bye, Grace," Caren said absently as the door chimes jingled.

She and Tate had been members of the Russelton
Cross-Country Ski Club for over two years. In the
summer they got enough exercise by swimming in the
lake and jogging along the beach, but their wintertime
activities tended to be pretty sedentary. The club had
offered an outlet for their physical energies as well as
a chance for Tate to meet the local residents. There
were usually two socials a year—one in the middle
of winter and one in early spring to wind everything
up. Caren sighed. It had been so long since she and
Tate had just gone out and had a good time together.
She would talk to him about the outing and see how
he felt. They were both so fragile at the moment.

"Did you sell something?" David called from the
back.

Caren slipped through the door. "Grace Stark bought
your casserole and matching soup bowls for Tony's
wedding."

"Her nephew?"

"Yes," Caren told him, returning to her place in
front of her wheel.

David grinned. "It's a good thing people keep getting married. Otherwise we'd be out of business."

"Oh-ho, you've certainly changed your tune in the
last few months," Caren teased. "You never used to
look on marriage so benignly."

"Someone had to hold out for bachelorhood."

"*Had* to? Does that mean you've changed your
mind? No more fears of mangled toothpaste tubes or
early-morning crankiness?"

David smiled secretly. "I've found someone who
likes to make love in the morning."

Caren laughed. "Great. I hope it works out for you.
Otherwise you'll end up a crusty old man."

David raised an eyebrow. "But I'll make lots of pots."

Caren laughed, dipping her fingers into the pail of water at her side and splashing the cylindrical clay form on her wheel. David turned on the radio, and with some lively pop music as background, they worked efficiently and quickly throughout the morning.

At noon the phone rang. David wiped his hands on a rag before picking up the receiver from the wall phone. "Hi," Caren heard him say. "Sure she's here." He handed her the receiver. "It's Tate."

"Hello," Caren said softly, wondering why her heart was pounding; but then Tate hadn't called the store for ages. Not that he had ever been one for long phone conversations, but he'd sometimes called just to say hello, to let her know she was in his thoughts.

"How are you doing?" he asked, his voice sounding husky and sexy over the line.

"I'm fine," she said breathlessly.

"It's snowing pretty hard out there," he said. "Have you had any customers?"

"Would you believe one?"

"Brave soul. By the way, I put some paint on a canvas this morning."

Caren detected a new note of animation and elation in his voice. She felt her own spirits soar at his words. "I'm glad, Tate." She glanced up as David walked into the front of the shop to give her some privacy. "Tell me about it. Did the inspiration just come to you, or what?"

He laughed. "I guess you could say that. I made some coffee and stared at the canvas, and I thought about a certain angelic muse. Next thing I knew I was mixing colors, slapping the paint on, and it just seemed to create itself."

"That's marvelous." Caren rubbed a finger over the black receiver, wishing she could touch her husband to show him she shared his excitement.

"Of course," he went on cautiously, "it's just a start."

"But that's the hardest part," she said encouragingly. "The way you're talking, it sounds as though the picture's already there. It's just a matter of transferring it from your soul to the canvas."

He gave an intimate chuckle. "You understand me so well, Caren. You really are my muse, angel."

His words were a precious gift. "I love you, Tate," she said softly, feeling that the words were inadequate to express the fullness of her emotion.

"And I love you. But I guess I'd better let you get back to work now."

"You mean *you* want to get back to work," she said teasingly. "Your fingers are just itching to get back to that canvas, aren't they?"

They laughed together, and then Caren said, "I'm glad you called, Tate."

"Me, too. See you tonight."

"I can't wait," she said. "Good-bye."

As she hung up the phone, tears flickered behind her eyes. She blinked them back automatically, but they were tears of joy. He was coming back to her.

She poked her head into the front of the shop. David was leafing through a supply catalogue. "I think I'll go out to the grocery store and get a sandwich," she said. "Do you want one?"

He glanced up. "Sure. What do they usually have?"

"Cheese or cheese," she said with a grin.

"I'll have the cheese."

Caren slipped into her coat and went along to pick up the sandwiches. The wind was howling and snow was whirling along the lakefront. It was twice as bad as it had been that morning. Her little car was tucked away by the side of the building, the blue roof peeping through the covering of snow.

At five-fifteen David helped Caren clear the snow from her car. As soon as she'd waved good night to him and he had trudged out of sight up the street to his home, she drove the car out of the lane and got stuck. Damn, damn, damn. Shovel in hand, she tried to make inroads into the snowdrift, but the blinding snow caught in her eyelids, and the wind froze her face. Each shovelful came blowing back into the drift.

She returned to the store. Should she alert Tate? She tried to dial home, but the phone was dead. Damn, damn, damn. She stood on the empty lakefront, frustrated, and began digging again. She didn't really want to be late two nights in a row. Tate had been so upset last night, even though it had worked out in the end. Still, she didn't want to endanger this precarious truce. Exhausted, she finally flung down the shovel.

She tried to phone home again, but the line was still dead. She filled the kettle, deciding to have some coffee before doing any more digging. As she sat waiting for the kettle to boil, her gloves drying over the edge of the counter, her stomach rumbled. She was hungry. She thought of the meal that Tate probably had ready, and her mouth watered. There was no food in the shop. Usually she kept a jar of cookies on hand, but it was empty except for crumbs. There was an old box of crackers on David's worktable. She munched on one and the salt made her thirsty. She took the kettle off the hot plate and made a cup of instant coffee.

She wished she weren't so hungry. She needed strength to dig the car out. She knew she could do it, but it would take time.

A banging at the front door made her tense, and she crept into the darkened storefront. It was Tate pressed up against the glass of the window. Greatly relieved, she opened the door and let him in.

"Your car stuck, ma'am?" he drawled.

"You'd better believe it," she said, throwing her arms around him. "I was trying to console myself with stale crackers."

"Ugh." He made a face, then drew her closer and kissed her hair. "Want me to dig?"

"If you wouldn't mind. I'll make you a cup of coffee while you do it."

She returned to the back room to prepare Tate's coffee. It didn't take him long to finish shoveling the car out. He came in, stamping his feet and breathing heavily.

"It's cold out there," he said. "Why didn't you call me?"

"The phones are dead down here. What made you decide to come down?" She hoped he wasn't still jealous of David, not after last night.

"I was worried about you. Scared to death, actually."

She heard the concern in his words and smiled gratefully as she handed him a cup of coffee. "Drink that. It'll warm you up."

"Are you glad I came?"

"Of course I'm glad you came. I might have been here all night."

"You still have the apartment upstairs, don't you?" He finished his coffee and put the cup on the counter.

"Yes, but I wasn't exactly looking forward to spending the night alone there. On the other hand, with you here..." She tossed off her jacket and flipped her hair over her shoulder. Her full breasts strained against the salmon-pink V-neck sweater, and her tight jeans outlined her hips and long legs. She licked her lips. "As a matter of fact, that bed hasn't been used since the day we moved my things over to the house. Remember, Tate?"

How could he forget the heaven she had promised that day? They hadn't been married then, but the delights he'd found with her made him eager for their wedding day. And now he felt that same eagerness for her. He was starved—hungry to the very core. Her breasts, taut against the sexy sweater, were almost too much. His eyes slipped to her shapely bottom.

She smoothed her hips with her palms, sensing his interest, feeling a current of desire flowing between them. "Come on, Tate."

The invitation was there. He moved toward her hurriedly and clasped her in his arms. Her mouth opened to greet his, and she slid her hands beneath his parka, over his shirt. "I love the feel of you," she whispered. "You're the only man for me. Make love to me, Tate."

He threw off his parka and lifted her into his arms. They took the little stairs to the apartment. Caren reached out to switch on the light as they went. Then she wrapped her arms around her husband's neck and dropped urgent kisses down his jaw to his mouth. "You need a shave," she chided.

"I was too worried about you to think of shaving."

She caressed his cheek. "I rather like it rough."

"Keep that up," he breathed in her ear, "and it will be rough."

She laughed, and he lowered her to her feet by the single bed. He tugged her sweater over her head. "I've been thinking about this all day."

"Me, too," she admitted, smoothing his dark straight hair, which was still a little damp. She found one stray snowflake and flipped it on to her finger. "It's like a fallen star."

He smiled. "You're like a little girl sometimes." He crushed her in his embrace. Then he unhooked her bra and freed her full breasts. He kissed each creamy globe reverently. "I think I'm going to paint you," he whispered. "I think I want to paint you."

"You said you'd never paint portraits," she whispered back, leaning into his arms and surrendering to the voluptuous sensations he was arousing in her flesh.

"There are portraits and then there's beauty. These are sheer beauty." He lifted her nipple to the tip of his tongue.

"Do you think it smells musty up here?" Caren asked suddenly.

"Who knows? I can only smell you," he breathed. "Your exotic perfume and soap, and . . . just you."

She buried her face in his chest, pressing her nose through the open buttons of his shirt. "Mmm, you smell good, too."

He clutched handfuls of her silken red hair and drew her face to his. His mouth covered hers, and Caren was lost. Clothes flew right and left. Naked, they sank down on the lumpy mattress. The yellow cotton cover felt cold, but they soon warmed it up. Tate's hands stroked her body, finding all her intimate pleasure spots and tantalizing her unmercifully.

Caren pulled herself to her knees, her body white in the glow from the dull light. She trailed her hair over his body until he groaned with delight. "You like that, Ashley?" she whispered, her mouth covering his body feverishly.

"You know it. I like everything you do."

"Tell me what you like," she murmured. "Everything."

He guided her, and she did things she'd never done before, and it pleasured and excited her. She was always amazed to find that each lovemaking experience could be so different, and all with the same man.

He rolled her over and pinned her down, leaning above her, his eyes glazed with desire and passion. "Now, Caren." He eased into her, filling her so wonderfully that she cried out. "I could stay here forever, Caren. This is where I belong."

"Don't leave, Tate," she begged, hugging him closer. They rocked in tandem with each other, the snowflakes became stars, and they both landed on a mattress of cloud.

There was no sound, only the wind rattling the little apartment windows. Caren shivered, suddenly realizing just how cold it was up here. Now she heard her sign creaking downstairs. Had they left the front door open? Real life began to filter in again. She sat up. "I'd better get dressed."

Tate had one leg thrown across the narrow bed, one dangling over the side. It had been built for a little girl, not a full-sized man. She laughed. "You look oversized for the bed," she told him, her hair tickling his navel as she leaned forward.

"I *am* oversized for the bed," he complained. "My feet stick out the end."

"Even I popped out as I grew older." She smiled. "Come on, I'm freezing, Tate. There's no heat up here."

"We found a good way to keep warm." He patted her bottom as she scrambled over him to look for her clothes.

As she got dressed, her stomach rumbled. "I'm starved," she complained, slipping her feet into her socks and boots. "Come on and get dressed, Ashley. Take me home."

"We might have to stay here all night." He made no move to leave as he watched her dress.

She gazed over his blatantly naked masculinity, loving the long, lean lines of his muscular body. "If I weren't so famished," she qualified, "I'd take you up on that."

"Haven't you got anything to eat in this place?"

"Nothing, and the restaurant up the road will be closed by now."

He stretched and yawned. "But I feel so good."

She knelt over him and caressed him boldly. "Your lady needs feeding, Tate."

He moved restlessly beneath her hands. "I dashed out to look for you without thinking about dinner. Do you want to eat at the hotel?"

"Shall we?" Her green eyes lit up. "I could have the fried chicken and chips, and salad, and apple pie, and . . ."

"Now *I'm* feeling hungry." He groaned. "Okay,

let's go to the hotel. I need a change from my cooking anyway."

As he dressed, Caren laughed. "You sound like a harried housewife. I guess it's time for me to start pulling my weight again in the kitchen."

He grinned. "No offense, but I'd rather you did the dishes and left the cooking to me."

She tossed the pillow at him and he ducked. Laughing, they raced down the stairs and slipped into their coats. They *had* left the door open. After turning off the lights, Caren locked it carefully. Her car was safely beside the store. She climbed into the Volkswagen van.

Caren had always liked Tate's van. There was a bunk bed, sink, and fridge in the back, and sometimes they took it into the bush to camp. They would huddle together, giggling on the narrow bed like a couple of children. Tate had lived and worked in the van at one time, and the pleasantly oily smell of paint had never quite left.

It had stopped snowing, and the streets were silent and soft. Tate drove up the hill out of town to the hotel. Located just off the highway, it was open all year round and always served good meals.

Caren brushed her hair and freshened her makeup in the rearview mirror before they left the van. She had a pleasant sense of anticipation as they walked together arm in arm. They really should get out more; she would talk to Tate about that shindig at the ski club.

From the outside the hotel looked like two rambling houses linked together by a long walkway. Maybe it had been at one time, Caren thought as they walked through the thick snow of the parking lot to the entrance. Inside the wooden foyer there was the delicious aroma of food and the musty smell of old homes. She didn't recognize the smiling waiter dressed in black pants and a crisp white shirt who led them into the dining room.

"Not very busy tonight," Tate said when he realized they were the only occupants.

The man smiled. "It's the weather. Glad you braved the elements anyway." He pulled out a chair with wooden arms for Caren.

She sat down, slipped off her jacket, and let it dangle over the back of the chair. "What are you going to have?" she asked Tate as they perused the menu.

"Chicken and chips—and all the other stuff you suggested earlier," he told her with a grin.

"Pig." She made a face at him.

"I'll work it all off shoveling snow," he promised.

They both ordered chicken and chips, salad, and apple pie and ice cream, but Tate had to eat some of Caren's pie when she gave up halfway through it.

"I thought you were starved," he said, taking her dish and pushing the pie onto his plate.

"I'm full now," she told him, sipping her coffee.

"It doesn't take much to keep you happy, does it?" He put down his fork. "An hour's good lovin'. A meal..."

"Does it make you happy, Tate?" she asked seriously, with a feeling that they were both forgetting about the underlying tension between them. It was almost as if they were ignoring the real problems in their relationship and working only on the more obvious symptoms.

"You know it does."

"We still have to talk. Maybe now we could pick up where we left off last night?"

"Caren, we can't discuss anything in here," he said, looking around.

"There's no one else here," she told him pointedly.

"The staff is probably all ears. These old places echo like hell."

"Then what do you want to do?"

"Go home," he said.

She stood up abruptly, tossing her brilliant red hair over her shoulder. "Fine with me." After shrugging into her jacket, she followed Tate out to the van.

When they were on the road, she said, "Last night you were blaming David for the rift between us. But there's something else, isn't there, Tate? I know there's something else. It has to do with the baby."

"There's nothing else," he snapped, not wanting to get into it. He had asked her last night to bear with him, had thought she understood. Now he felt she was pressuring him, saying the start they'd made wasn't enough for her. That *he* wasn't enough for her.

"If there's nothing else, then why do I get the impression that you're holding out on me?" Caren persisted. "Is it something to do with your work, Tate? Do you have some kind of a block? You can discuss it with me, darling..."

"Please, Caren. Let things ride for a while. We've had an emotional two days. Let's keep it cool."

He turned the van up the driveway and they plowed to the end, Tate intently navigating through the thick snow, and Caren keeping silent to let him concentrate. They parked in the garage and went into the house.

Caren took off her coat and boots and climbed the

stairs to brush her hair and wash her hands while Tate made up the fire. She looked through her books and picked out one she'd been meaning to read for a while. Then she went downstairs and sat cross-legged by the fireplace, watching the dancing orange flames as they began to ignite the fresh logs. She wasn't sure what it was between them. The sexual pressure had been released, and the tension in the atmosphere had snapped like a broken rubber band. But she was sure Tate was still keeping something from her. Something really serious.

Maybe he didn't love her. Maybe he had only wanted to make love. Or maybe it was what she'd always feared—that Tate was waiting for her to get pregnant again, and if it didn't happen, then he wouldn't want her anymore. That would account for his passionate lovemaking and subsequent withdrawal.

She leaned back into the cushions. How she wished she knew a little more about him. Oh, she knew the usual things: some incidents in his childhood, a relationship with a girl named Lisa. She knew his parents, too. His mother, Donna, was a sweet, dark-haired woman, interested in the arts. Certainly a strange match for his brash, bustling father, George. And his older brothers, Harry and Ron, were like his father. Tate was the odd one out. He admitted it and accepted it. At least he did now. Caren didn't think that had always been the case.

Three years married and she had thought she knew him so well, but she was only on the threshold of understanding. It would take a lifetime to really get to know him, and she wanted to be sure she'd have that lifetime. She didn't want it torn away prematurely. She didn't want their marriage to end in divorce. *Divorce.* She couldn't even think of the word without getting an icy-cold feeling inside.

A sinking sensation overtook her when she considered what life would be like without Tate. She now understood how her mother must have felt when her father had suffered a sudden, fatal heart attack. Losing a spouse, under any circumstances, must be like having half of your self ripped away. These past few months had been the most painful in Caren's experience. And Tate had still been with her, at least physically.

No. She was going to fight for this twosome even if it meant divesting herself of all pride. If, in the end, he really didn't love her, then she would let him go.

Not sure of his mood since their abrupt departure from the restaurant, Caren smiled cautiously at Tate as he entered the room carrying more wood for the fire. But he seemed okay and knelt down beside her on the rug to sort the logs. He put a couple of the smaller ones on the fire and left the larger ones in the bin for another night.

He sat back on the rug with her, determined to make amends for their argument in the restaurant. "What are you reading?"

Caren picked up the book that she hadn't even opened. "It's a mystery story that takes place in Quebec. I've heard it's pretty good."

"Might be interesting." He picked up her left hand and linked it with his. Their matching gold wedding bands gleamed in the glow from the fire. He touched her hand to his lips. "Want to take a bath?"

She looked into his dark blue eyes, and her mouth trembled beneath his passionate gaze. "Sounds interesting," she whispered.

"I'll make it interesting," he promised.

"You've got a date." She squeezed his fingers. "With bubbles or without?"

He grinned. "Bubbles, of course."

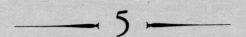

# 5

CAREN CAME AWAKE with Tate kissing her eyelids. "What is it?" she asked. She hadn't slept so well in months, and she felt rested and satisfied.

"We're snowed in," he whispered.

"You're kidding."

"You should look outside."

Caren did just that. She leaped from the bed, her slim white body exciting Tate as he watched her. She gazed out the window at a completely white world. And the snow was still whirling and twirling down from the sky. It was a blizzard, much worse than yesterday's snowstorm.

She gazed mischievously at Tate, who lay naked on the bed, his body looking big and masculine. "What are we going to do all day?"

"Guess," he said, grinning.

*"All* day?"

"Well, not all day. I'd better get on with that painting I started. It's kind of eating at me now. Come here."

She joined him on the bed and slipped her arms around his waist. They kissed, and she found the hunger that had been satiated last night returning in full force. They slid together, both surprised to find that their lovemaking was short and fierce this morning. Afterward, they lay panting beside each other and then laughed simultaneously.

"Short and very, very sweet," Tate said.

"Mm. And for a follow-up, how about bacon and eggs, and pan-fries, and toast?" she suggested. "I'll even cook it—breakfasts I can manage," she told him, and scampered from the bed.

Caren showered and dressed in jeans and an old blue sweater. She didn't have to go to work today. It felt good. In fact, she felt delirious. She hummed little songs, mixing all sorts of tunes as she cooked their breakfast. She heard the shower go on upstairs, and it gave her a warm feeling to know that Tate would be coming down to her, smiling again.

They ate the pile of food at the kitchen table, bringing up remembrances of their married life, laughing over dumb things they'd done. And yet they avoided talking about the baby. Every issue skirted around September and the tragedy that had pulled them apart. Their newly repaired bond was still very fragile, Caren reflected as she washed the dishes and Tate went to work on his painting, but they had made a start. A very healthy start.

Caren phoned the shop to find that David had arrived. "As you probably know, I can't get out of my house," she told him. "I'll get Tate to drive me in tomorrow to dig out my car again."

David laughed. "I had to crawl through the back window and then shovel the snow away from the door afterward. It was piled high. I'm keeping the shop closed. I talked to the shipping company, and they might not be able to come out until next week."

"Damn," Caren said. "You know, I just might take a trip down to London and deliver some of that stuff myself. I wouldn't mind a day away from Russelton."

"Who wouldn't?" David said wryly. "That's a good idea, though."

"I think so, too," Caren said, but another idea was forming in her mind. A very important idea, concerning Tate. "Anyhow," she continued, "I won't be in today, obviously. Don't work too hard."

"I'll think of you cozy at home." David laughed before he hung up.

Tate seemed to be working hard in his studio and Caren went upstairs into the spare room. It was a mess. She pushed up her sleeves. What better than a snowy day off to do something about it.

The room was full of boxes of memorabilia that she had never bothered to unpack when she moved in with Tate. She sat on her knees to sort through it all, laughing at some things, feeling a lump of nostalgia over others. She threw out what she didn't want and repacked the rest in boxes which she stored in the spacious closet. Then she plugged in Tate's old black and white television, but all she managed to get was a very fuzzy picture and crackly sound. She put the TV away with the boxes.

Caren had lost all track of time, and she was startled

when Tate popped his head around the door and said, "I've made sandwiches and coffee. Feel like lunch?"

"That sounds great," she said enthusiastically. "I'm cleaning up this room."

"Good for you. It's good to see you taking an interest again."

"I guess I've been a real drag lately," Caren mused.

He shrugged his broad shoulders beneath the black cotton shirt. "It wasn't your fault. Any woman would have been upset."

"But I'm not any woman, Tate. I'm Caren Bryant Ashley, and I'm not normally like that."

He put out his hand, and she took it and jumped to her feet.

"Don't dwell on it too much," he said. "Let's just build on what we've got."

Caren sighed as she walked downstairs with him. "I know, but I've always believed that the root of any problem should be solved because just glossing over things doesn't do any good."

"I agree with you," he said. "It's like juvenile delinquency. They punish the kids but never try to understand *why* they're like that."

"You're right. Were you a juvenile delinquent, Tate?"

He glanced at her. "Not in the usual sense, but there were leanings in that direction because I was so dissatisfied with what was being offered within the school system and at home."

"And I was the opposite," she said. "I just took everything as gospel. Nothing worried me. I didn't fight."

"And yet you like to fight," he reminded her.

"I'd like to claw your eyes out sometimes," she

said. "Especially when you get moody and look at me without really seeing me."

"That's my protection." He urged her down into a chair at the kitchen table and placed a ham and cheese sandwich on thick rye bread in front of her. He sat opposite and poured two mugs of coffee. "The only one in my family who ever understood my needs was my mother. We got along real well, but she couldn't say anything bad about Dad. She loved him. Still loves him, I guess. My brothers were big, brash people. I was their little kid brother who did dumb things like read serious books and paint pictures." He bit into his sandwich.

Caren laughed, glancing over his broad shoulders and wide chest. "Little brother?"

"I was kind of skinny when I was a kid," he admitted. "Anyhow, I used to clam up against them all. It was a case of staying on the outer circle. 'If you can't fight 'em, join 'em' was never my motto. I wanted to be different. Inside I knew I was different."

"Do your brothers have good marriages?" Caren asked thoughtfully. She had only met his family a few times, and on those occasions there hadn't been time for anything more than small talk.

"I think Harry and Mary are pretty well settled, but Ron and Laura have their problems. Ron's always had a wandering eye. I don't think he's been faithful to her."

"What about your dad?"

"With my mom? As far as I could tell, there was no hanky-panky, but what do kids ever really know about their parents?"

"Your mom's so pretty," Caren said. "I shouldn't think your father would want to stray."

"I really don't think he has. He put an awful lot of energy into that construction business. I never wanted to be part of it, but I admire him for his sticking power. Not that we ever talked much."

"Poor Tate," she murmured. "Daddy doesn't understand you."

She had been teasing. She didn't expect his violent reaction. He stood up suddenly and turned his back to her.

"Tate?" she questioned.

"I'm going back to work," he said, and walked out of the kitchen.

"You haven't finished your sandwich," she called, standing by the door, wondering what was wrong. Why should the mention of his dad trigger such an emotional response? She knew Tate and his father had had their disagreements, but she'd assumed that was all in the past. Lately, the two men had been doing their best to be conciliatory.

Tate stood by his easel, squeezing tubes of paint onto the piece of masonite board he used as his palette.

"Tate, what is it?"

"Nothing." He shrugged. "I'm not hungry."

Then Caren came and stood behind him where he was working, something she rarely did. The painting on the easel took her breath away. What she saw on the canvas excited her. A child seemed to be magically ascending to the sky, while men and women reached up to bring it back to earth, but the child escaped their grasping fingers. It was a mystical, powerful, picture, with startling harmonies of color and striking composition. It wasn't a painting in the realistic mode, and yet it wasn't quite abstract either. It was Tate

Ashley as he'd been at the peak of his success back in his late twenties.

"What's it called?" she asked in a half-whisper.

"I thought of calling it *Breakaway*," he said. "What do you think?"

"It's fantastic. I love it." Caren grew more and more enthusiastic as she walked back and forth to survey the painting. It was far from finished, but it was spellbinding. The images drew her mind through some interesting and thought-provoking patterns. But one question stood out in her mind: Was the child Tate? If so, then the grasping hands must belong to his own family. His reaction just a moment ago when she'd teased him about his father had been dramatic. He'd never told her much about his family; was this his own subconscious story?

She watched him study her reaction, and she smiled softly. He had begun to work again. She didn't want to cause him any turmoil, and quickly decided against discussing the hidden meanings of the picture. "It's beautiful, Tate. Your work has always excited me."

"It's what you do to me," he admitted, his earlier discomfort apparently forgotten.

She stood on tiptoe to kiss him, then rubbed her cheek against his. The idea she'd had when talking on the phone to David this morning was starting to take form. "I'll bring the rest of your lunch to the studio. That way you can keep working."

Caren wiled away the rest of the afternoon in the spare room. By four o'clock she had a roast beef and vegetables in the oven, and the room was tidy and clean. She even fitted a pair of bright red curtains to the window.

The snow had finally stopped. A soft luminescence lay over the gray lake and hilly landscape as the sun made its first appearance of the day only to immediately begin its descent for the night. To work up an appetite for dinner, Tate and Caren dressed warmly and went outside to shovel snow from in front of the house. By the time they had finished, they were both breathing heavily. Caren flung herself down in a snow drift.

"I'm sweltering," she groaned.

"I've got a cure for that." Tate grinned, picking up some snow and packing it between his gloved hands.

"Oh, no," she squealed, but she was too late. Snow trickled in icy clumps down the back of her neck. Tate pinned her down on the snowbank and kissed her.

"I want to make love to you," he told her, nipping her nose with his teeth.

"Out here?"

"Why not?"

"Won't you shrivel up?"

"Don't insult me! I never shrivel up."

Caren giggled. Soon she was laughing so hard she could hardly contain herself. Tate joined in. Before Caren could figure out how it happened, they were both rolling around in the snow.

"I'm freezing," she moaned.

"And I'm hungry," he said. "Come on, sweetheart. Help me up."

At dinner, Tate reminisced about the days when he had lived and painted in the van. She had heard much of this before, but Tate had added some new and quite hilarious material to his repertoire. The lighthearted mood that had begun with their romp in the snow was still with them, and they continued to burst into laughter periodically. Tate told her about the time he had parked for the night and suddenly heard a scampering sound. Convinced there was a skunk inside, he'd run naked from the van. When he finally saw it was only a chipmunk, he felt like a fool. Fortunately, he finished with a grin, he'd been camping in the bush, far from the regular campgrounds.

"I can just see it." She laughed, holding her sides. "Oh, Tate, help!"

He lifted her into his arms and carried her to the cushions by the fireplace. He stretched out beside her on the rug and dropped light, feathery kisses onto her lips. "Still worried that I'll shrivel up?"

"What? I can't feel anything." Caren giggled, moving her body against his insistent hardness.

"You'll feel something soon. I promise you." He stripped them both of their clothing, and immediately they began to thrash wildly together.

"Tate, I can't stand it!" Caren gasped. The delicious sensations were just too intense.

Tate slowed his rhythms, but soon Caren was clinging to him, begging for more.

"You want more?" He grinned. "More?"

"More," she insisted. "I'll never accuse you of being shriveled up again."

"You'd better not." And then he made love to her again; and again. Caren's passions ebbed and flowed deep into the night. Where had her sexuality been hiding itself? She had always had a healthy appetite for lovemaking, but nothing like this. When Tate ended his assault, they rolled away from each other, exhausted.

"Married people aren't supposed to do this, are they?" Caren mumbled. "I thought it was supposed to get boring after a while."

"It gets better every time, doesn't it?" Tate said.

"I'll sleep like a log tonight." She curled up on the cushions. "In fact, I think I'll just sleep here."

With a contented smile, Tate roused himself to close down the house and get a blanket. Then he cuddled down beside Caren and drew her close. He closed his eyes. This was the life.

Caren spent the next few days at Caren's Crafts eager to get home to Tate, her lover, her husband. She sang as she worked, and her step was sprightly as she moved around the shop.

"Things must be going well on the homefront," David said casually one afternoon. He was glazing a large fruit bowl a beautiful shade of gold.

She smiled serenely. "Better every day."

David nodded. "Snowstorms come in handy sometimes."

"I'll say." Caren smiled secretly. "You know, David, the weather's so good now, I think I'll drive down to London tomorrow and deliver that stuff. The shipping company can still pick up the merchandise for the Toronto stores."

"Fine," David said. "Want me to come along?"

They had gone together a few times, but right now, her relationship with Tate on a precarious pinnacle, Caren thought she'd better go alone. In fact, she wanted to go alone.

"I'd prefer to go by myself," she said at last. "Thanks for the offer, though." She stood up and went through to the shop where she flipped open her address book and found the name she was looking for. A few minutes later the phone was ringing in the Wyatt Gallery in London, Ontario.

"Hello, Wyatt," a woman's voice answered.

"Tanya, this is Caren Ashley."

"Caren, how lovely. I haven't seen or heard from you in ages. How's Tate?"

"He's pretty good. I'm coming down to London tomorrow. I thought maybe lunch might be in order. Don't I owe you?"

"Probably." Tanya laughed. "But we'll sort that out when you get here. I'd love to see you. Is it business or pleasure?"

"A bit of both," Caren admitted. "It's about Tate." She might as well be honest from the beginning.

"Is he coming with you?"

"No, I don't think so. I have a proposition to make."

"Sounds intriguing," Tanya mused. "Okay then, Caren. Tomorrow around noon?"

"That's fine," Caren agreed, and hung up. She rested her chin against an open palm and leaned on the counter. Tanya had given Tate his first show when he was eighteen. Although at that time Tanya had run her own small gallery, she had since paired up with her husband, Ben Wyatt, to form one of the best galleries in London. Tate always had a few paintings there for sale, and once in a while a check would come through; but since Tate hadn't produced much lately, the checks were few and far between. Besides, Tate needed a one-man show. Something he could work toward, something that would give him renewed confidence in his work. Tate would never arrange a show for himself, but if he thought there was a demand for one . . .

She approached him at dinner with her plan to drive down to London to deliver the crafts.

"Are you going to drive there and back in one day?" he asked, looking worried.

"Maybe not. Shall I stay with your parents?"

"Why don't you. I'm sure Mom would love to see you."

"Then I'll do it. I haven't seen them since Christmas."

"I'd come with you," Tate said, "but I want to get this painting finished."

"That's fine." She was glad he couldn't come. Her plans might be stymied if he did.

Later that evening they phoned Donna Ashley and told her Caren would be coming the following evening.

"I'll have a meal ready for you about six," Donna said. "I'll look forward to it."

Caren had one more chore to perform. When Tate went out to the garage to check her car in preparation for the trip to London, she pulled out her Polaroid camera. She took three color photographs of Tate's new painting, *Breakaway,* and put them in an envelope in her purse. She didn't want Tate to know what she was doing just yet. He might object and cause a scene, whereas if she made it seem the suggestion had come from Tanya—well, Tate needed that kind of ego boost.

She packed a small zippered bag with her green nightgown and a matching robe, underwear, and a clean blouse. She was ready to leave before they went to bed.

They cuddled down together beneath the orange comforter.

"Things okay now, Caren?" Tate asked, stroking her hair.

"Not bad. What about you?"

"I feel better, freer in a sense. I'll miss you tomorrow, darling."

"You can continue to work all night without me interrupting," she told him, kissing his strong throat. She wrapped her arms tighter around him. "I love you, Tate."

"I love you too, baby. I always will, you know that."

"I hope so." Caren let out a long emotional sigh. "I was thinking about our wedding, Tate, reminiscing a little."

"The ceremony, or that chintzy motel down near Buffalo?" He laughed. "I thought we'd end up stabbed to death in our beds."

"We were quite an act ourselves. Can we go there again?"

"Not to that motel."

"No, silly, to the lakes and to the ocean."

"Maybe in the spring."

"I'd like that. We could take the van and camp." Caren closed her eyes sleepily. "Sounds good, Ashley."

He kissed her. "Sleepy?"

"Got anything better in mind?" Her speech was slurred with fatigue.

Tate closed his eyes. "Not tonight, Josephine."

She giggled and then gradually drifted off to sleep in his arms.

Caren was up early the next morning. She dressed in jeans tucked into tan western boots and a green flannel shirt. The car was packed with the boxes of pottery to be delivered and her overnight bag. The sun was shining brightly from a blue sky, and the snow was crisp and clean.

"Spring's in the air," she told Tate as they stood beside the car.

"You're nuts." He smiled. "It's only January. This is Canada, remember?"

"I'm already thinking of our vacation down south." She pulled the zipper on her jacket and straightened her jeans. "How do I look?"

Tate tugged her white knit hat down over her ears. "Good enough to eat. Phone me tonight from Mom's?"

"Definitely. Although maybe you'd better call me. You know how your dad feels about long-distance telephone calls."

"He's cheap," Tate agreed. "Okay, I'll call you. Are you going to drop in on Tanya and Ben?"

Caren almost flushed guiltily, but she smiled instead. "That's a good idea. Maybe they'll buy me lunch."

"You probably owe them."

"They're richer than I am," she said mischievously, and then looked at her waiting car. "I'd better go, honey. Good-bye."

They kissed lingeringly, and then Tate stood back. He was wearing only a black sweat shirt and jeans, and it was a chilly morning. Caren could see their breath mingling in the clear air.

She slipped into the car and turned the ignition key. The engine had already been warmed up while she was having her last cup of coffee, and now it jumped to life easily.

Tate saluted, and Caren drove off down the driveway. The highway was clear of snow, and she rode along with the radio playing an upbeat tune, feeling lighthearted and optimistic.

At Exeter she picked up Highway 4 and sailed along peacefully. Snowbanks and spindly, naked trees dotted the roadsides, and sprawling snow-covered fields basked beneath the brilliant sun and blue sky.

When she saw a sign for London, she felt quite excited. The closest urban center to Russelton, it had always been the big city for her. She had a lot of friends here, men and women who had moved away from Russelton, but she wouldn't be visiting them today. She had more important things to do.

# 6

IT WAS GOOD to get into the city. London was a busy industrial center with a major university, but still it retained a small-town flavor. It was situated on the Thames River, and many of its street names were reminiscent of their namesakes from London, England, a city Caren had always yearned to visit. The river meandered through the heart of the city, providing a picturesque backdrop for the numerous trees, well-maintained streets, and large old houses.

Caren always enjoyed the excellent museums, galleries, and parks the small city had to offer. She recalled an early visit with Tate to Springbank Park when they had strolled over some of the 350 acres of flower-dotted lawns on the banks of the Thames. They had taken a cruise on a paddlewheeler, *The Storybook*

*Queen,* and wondered if they would ever bring their children to the theme park, Storybook Gardens.

Maybe one day, Caren thought now, and was surprised at herself. Perhaps her natural resiliency was resurfacing. For the first time since the miscarriage, the thought of getting pregnant again didn't upset her.

Caren had deliveries to make at five specialty stores. She chatted awhile with each of the owners, and in one case stayed for a cup of coffee, but managed to finish her calls by lunchtime. She parked her car on the street close to the Wyatt Gallery, which was in an old, three-story orange-brick house in a commercially zoned area. Purse over her shoulder, Caren walked quickly along the sidewalk against the winter chill and into the warm gallery.

Ben Wyatt, a bear of a man with curly gray hair and full beard, was setting up a display of silver-framed pastel watercolors.

"Well, if it isn't Caren! How are you? Tanya's just getting herself prettied up for your luncheon date."

"Oh, dear." Caren laughed. "And I've just come in my old jeans and shirt."

"You look lovely as usual." Ben's eyes twinkled. "How's Tate?"

"He's doing pretty well. He's painting again."

"Again? Did he go through a rough spell?"

"Unfortunately, yes. You know what Tate's like."

"He's a real perfectionist, too much so for his own good. But it's an occupational hazard, I guess. I've got three artists stuck in the doldrums now. One's getting a divorce, one can't decide what he wants to paint, and the third, a lovely lady, is getting married and on the verge of nervous collapse over that."

Caren laughed. "Artists are so fragile."

"You can say that again. How's the shop?"

"Coming along fine."

"And David? He was in here a few weekends ago with a pretty brunette on his arm. I can't remember her name. It's hard to keep up with all his women."

Caren smiled. "David's fine."

"He's a good potter. You know, Tanya and I have been thinking of putting a bit of pottery around the gallery."

"We'll supply some," Caren offered immediately, always on the lookout for new markets.

"You'll be the first one we'll ask to supply us." Ben grinned and then nodded as his wife came down the back stairs. Tanya and Ben lived on the top two floors of the old place, which was now modernized inside beyond recognition. Tanya's flair for decorating was apparent throughout the house. At this time the living quarters were decorated in red and white, and the gallery in silver and green. There was a steady stream of customers, and the Wyatts seemed to live quite comfortably. Ben always said it was because he was a good salesman, but Caren knew there'd been money from Tanya's family to start the business.

Tanya herself was a rather wild lady, and Caren loved her. She was in her late thirties and had a shock of curly auburn hair. Today her tall, willowy figure was clothed in black silk pants, matching shirt, and high-heeled leather boots.

Caren glanced down at her own tan western boots, her only concession to current fashion.

"Caren, you look lovely." Tanya smiled when she saw her. "Look at that beautiful hair, Ben. I don't know how Tate can resist painting it."

"He manages. You're looking terrific yourself, Tanya."

"Thanks." Tanya smiled her acceptance of the compliment as she picked up a short fake-fur jacket in dark brown and black stripes. "We're going down to the oyster bar, sweetheart," she told her husband. "Can you manage with a sandwich?"

"I guess I'll have to." Ben looked forlorn. "I'd come with you, but I have to hang this show," he explained to Caren. "We're opening tonight at eight."

"See you later, then," Caren called as Tanya ushered her out of the gallery. They began walking down the street at a brisk pace.

"We've been so busy lately," Tanya said with a sigh.

"It gets that way," Caren agreed.

Tanya led her guest into a dark little oyster bar. Once seated in a narrow corner booth, she smiled and said, "You don't have to have oysters. They have other fish. The trout is delicious."

"I'll have trout and a Perrier and lime," Caren said, closing the menu.

Tanya also ordered a Perrier, along with the oysters, which were served raw and heavily seasoned and made Caren flinch.

They chatted for a while about family matters, Caren catching up on the news of Tanya's mother, who also ran a gallery, in New York. Then Tanya slipped an oyster into her mouth and said, "Okay, shoot. What's Tate up to?"

"I'd like you to promise him a show. Maybe in a few months' time."

"What's he working on?"

Caren opened her purse and drew out the colored photographs of *Breakaway*. "This kind of thing."

Tanya glanced at the pictures thoughtfully. It was a long time before she looked back at Caren, and by then Caren's breath was caught somewhere in her throat.

"This looks pretty good. Of course, I really should see the original. Has he got more?"

"He's got hundreds of blank canvases, and I think he will fill more of them."

Tanya raised her eyebrows. "I presume he hasn't been doing much?"

"We've had problems," Caren said, and then launched into a brief explanation.

Tanya looked sympathetic. "I'm sorry, I didn't know. But I do know about Tate's moods. Look Caren, I'd like to give Tate a show, but there must be enough pictures to make it worthwhile. I've known Tate since he was seventeen. He's a creative genius—I'm not disputing that—but he has his on and off periods. Sometimes he's all fired up and painting like mad, and other times he's down in the dumps and doing nothing. I've given him enough meals and put enough dollar bills in his back pocket to keep him afloat through some long dry spells."

Caren leaned across the table. "Tanya, he needs a show. He has to have something to work for. He's out of the woods now, I promise you. He just did this painting the other day and evening. It's really fantastic Tanya. It's Tate as he was at his peak."

"He's still at his peak," Tanya amended. "His paintings are always in demand. If I had a hundred, I could sell them all. He'd sell out a show. But I don't want to book the space, advertise, and then have him pull out on me. It wouldn't be good for my reputation, or for his."

"He won't," Caren assured her. "I'll keep him at it."

"He's pulled out on me before, Caren." Tanya sighed. "I'm not saying he hasn't made money for me . . . Okay, we'll give it a try. Can Ben and I come up to see his stuff?"

"How much do you want to see?"

"As much as he has. The original of *Breakaway*, of course, and whatever else he can produce before we arrive."

"You can come up next weekend," Caren said. "But arrange something first with Tate. I think he needs encouragement."

Tanya smiled. "I know. It's such a lonely business, and Tate fights his aloneness. Okay, what I'll do is call him and then follow it up with a letter, tentative dates, and all that. I'll mention we'll be coming up to see his work."

"Tate and I would love to have you stay the night," Caren said, excited by the thought of having Tanya and Ben for a whole weekend.

"That would be fun," Tanya agreed. "Ben would like a weekend in the country, and we'd enjoy seeing Tate again."

Caren touched Tanya's hand, noticing how slim it was beneath the heavy silver rings. "I'm really grateful, Tanya."

"You needn't be. I wouldn't be doing this if I didn't think Tate could come through for us. I have confidence in Tate—especially with you behind him. You're the best thing that ever happened to Tate,

Caren. Before you came along, I sometimes thought he was intent on destroying himself."

"From what he tells me, you were his mentor in the early years," Caren said, touched by Tanya's words.

Tanya nodded. "He was a good kid with a fantastic talent and the tenacity to pull it off. I was happy to give him all the encouragement I could."

Caren smiled slightly. "You're not much older than Tate."

"Enough so that when he was seventeen I was already finished with college and running a gallery. Lucky for him."

"I'm glad he found you," Caren agreed.

"And I'm glad he found you. I'm not saying any of this lightly, Caren. I really am fond of Tate."

"I know."

Tanya peered at her empty glass. "Want some coffee or something?"

"Sounds good."

They sat for another hour, dawdling over their coffee as they chatted about art trends, crafts, the state of the economy, and anything else that seemed to pop up. Caren finally left Tanya at the gallery door with their plans confirmed.

"Don't let on to Tate that this was my idea," Caren cautioned her friend.

"I won't. Can I keep the photographs to show Ben?"

"Of course."

"Then I'll see you soon, Caren. Tate will be hearing from me." Tanya leaned over to kiss her cheek. "Take care. "Are you driving home tonight?"

"No. I'm staying with Tate's mom and dad."

"Lucky you. George will be able to tell you what

a waste of time it is being an artist or a potter."

Caren laughed. "I don't listen. Thanks for lunch, by the way."

"You're welcome. We'll be seeing you."

Tanya swept away, and Caren walked slowly to her car. She still had a few hours to kill and decided to browse through some of her favorite antique stores. By the time she finished, it was nearly six o'clock, and she drove quickly to the huge, old-fashioned mansion that was the Ashley home. It was set well back from a street lined with large trees. The lawns were wide, but of course they were covered with snow at this time of year.

Caren parked in the circular driveway behind George Ashley's brown Buick. As she took her overnight bag from the car and climbed the steps to the front door, she felt a little apprehensive. She had never visited the house without Tate. Although she had always gotten along well with his mother, they'd never had a chance to really get to know one another. She rang the doorbell, feeling rather small and insignificant, as she usually did when she came to this house. She suspected that Tate must have found it rather overwhelming as a child.

Donna Ashley came to the door, a smile on her face. She had black hair, the same as Tate's, which she wore short and wavy. A few attractive streaks of gray showed at her temples. Her skin was smooth, and her aristocratic features were similar to Tate's, as were her blue eyes. Tall and slim in high heels, black pants, and a gray silk blouse, she was an elegant woman.

"Caren, dear. It's lovely to see you." She whisked her daughter-in-law into the warm foyer. "Wasn't it a lovely sunny day?"

"Beautiful," Caren agreed with a smile as she put her bag on the polished parquet floor by the radiator in the front hall. Pale rust carpet took over where the floor left off, covering the downstairs rooms, the wide oak bannistered staircase and landing. Caren remembered that Tate had told her how he used to slide down those bannisters. One day he'd gone flying off and hit his head on the crystal chandelier that hung low in the center of the hall. Caren nearly giggled thinking about it now, but said, "How are you, Donna?" Tate's mother had insisted from the beginning that they be on a first-name basis.

"I'm keeping well. How are you, dear?" Donna looked her over with an anxious expression.

"I'm much better now," Caren assured her. "In fact, I'm fine."

"I'm so glad. Here, let me take your things. And how's Tate?" As she spoke, she hung Caren's jacket in the wide hall closet.

"Tate's doing well," Caren said. "He sends his love."

"Dear boy. I haven't seen him for a while. Next time you come, bring him along."

"He's working hard," Caren said. "That's really why he didn't come." She followed Donna into the living room. Bay windows overlooked long landscaped gardens. Snow covered the trelliswork and lawns, but in summer the area would be a picture of bright roses and lush trees and shrubs. A little wooden gazebo was set to one side of the lawn.

Another of Tate's memories intruded. When he was a little boy, he'd hidden his first drawings in the gazebo beneath a boulder because his father hadn't wanted them in the house. Eventually his mother found out what was going on and changed his father's attitude—or at least the rules and regulations. From then on, Tate was allowed to draw in the house. Once she'd heard that story, Caren had found it very difficult to like George Ashley.

"Well," Donna said, smiling, "I'm glad to hear Tate's working. He gets so moody when he's in a slump. I think he feels he should be working at fever pitch all the time. He doesn't give himself time to calm down and collect himself."

"You're probably right." Caren seated herself on the green velvet sofa.

"Would you like something to drink? I have some nice dry sherry."

"That would be good," Caren said. "I lunched with Tanya Wyatt this afternoon."

"And how's she? Such a crazy lady, but she did Tate a world of good." Donna went to the bar to pour two sherries from a cut-glass decanter. She handed Caren her drink and sat down on the armchair opposite.

"Tanya's fine. Full of amusing anecdotes, as always." Caren decided not to mention the show yet, until it was confirmed with Tate. She didn't want to embarrass him if it didn't materialize.

"Sounds like fun. By the way, George is upstairs showering and changing. He'll be down in a minute."

"Fine," Caren said, but she tensed a little at the thought of Tate's father. He had an abrupt manner that always made her somewhat nervous.

"Actually, Caren," Donna said hesitantly, "much as I'd like to see Tate, I'm rather glad you're here by yourself this time. You know I couldn't have been more delighted when you and Tate got married, and

I always hoped you and I would be close. But we see each other all too seldom, and then mostly at big family get-togethers with no opportunity for a good long talk. The problem is, both George and Tate like to stay on their own turf."

"You're right," Caren agreed. "Now that I'm here, I wonder why I've never just come down by myself before. I've wanted to get to know you better, too, Donna, especially with my own mother dead. You know, after I lost the baby I was very depressed, and somehow I had the feeling that if I could only talk to you about it, I'd feel much better. But at Christmas, with Tate's brother and their families here, there was never a chance to talk to you privately."

"Oh, my dear," Donna said sympathetically, reaching out and giving Caren's hand a small squeeze. "I feel so terrible. When Tate told us about the miscarriage, my first instinct was to go to you, but George wouldn't hear of my leaving him for a few days, and..."

Her voice trailed off, but Caren finished the sentence in her own head: *I thought it would only make matters worse if George and I came together.* Caren knew then that the tension between Tate and his father went very deep, and she decided that at some point during this visit she would ask Donna for a clarification of that relationship.

Just then, a movement by the door made Donna glance up. "Oh, George, Caren's here."

George Ashley was an impressive and intimidating figure. Caren could see how he had made a success of his business. He was wearing a blue knit pullover with a crew neck and long sleeves, and casual gray pants. He was well over six feet tall, with broad shoulders and a stomach that was beginning to get paunchy. His hair was wavy and dark, flecked with gray and very distinguished. Grayish-brown eyebrows frowned over pale blue eyes and a short nose. His rounded jaw had been inherited by Harry and Ron but certainly not by Tate, who always gave the impression of leanness. Nevertheless, Caren saw some of Tate in his father. It was less a resemblance of feature than a similarity of character. They shared the same determination and stubbornness, the same drive to do well in life. George Ashley came from a poor family, and he had fought against being poor himself. He had certainly succeeded in that, Caren thought.

He came forward on the soft carpet, stretching out his hand. "How are you, dear?"

"I'm fine," Caren said, and was surprised when he leaned down to kiss her cheek.

"You look a bit better. You were very pale last time we saw you. How's Tate?"

"He's very well, thanks," Caren told him. "He sends his love." He hadn't, but she thought he should have.

"You can send mine back to him," George said gruffly, and then, as if feeling awkward, he turned to his wife. "Donna, is that meal ready? I'm hungry."

"It's all ready. I was just letting Caren relax and have her drink."

"I'm fine." Caren stood up. "Let's eat."

She followed Tate's mother and father into the large dining room, which overlooked the back lawns and gardens. Crystal and silverware shone from the white linen placemats on the long polished mahogany table. Luckily, they all sat grouped at one end and didn't have to shout at each other to talk.

George discussed his business, explaining it in great detail. Caren had heard all about the construction company many times before, and as usual George voiced his desire for Tate to come into the business.

"You'd have a much more steady living," he told Caren. "You wouldn't have to hide yourself away in the bush."

"We're not exactly hiding," Caren said. She had realized at a very early stage that one resisted George Ashley or got trampled. She understood Tate's motives exactly. "Besides, I have my shop."

"You wouldn't have to work. Tate would be an executive."

The thought of Tate as an executive for a construction company almost made Caren laugh out loud. And she couldn't see herself in a home like this, entertaining the Ashleys' business associates. "I love my work. It's important to me," she said.

"Come on, George," Donna protested. "Tate has his life, and Caren is perfectly content doing her thing. Don't hector them."

"But Ron and Harry are doing so well. Do you know that Harry's going to buy a three-hundred-thousand-dollar home with an indoor and outdoor swimming pool, Caren?"

"We have an entire lake," she pointed out softly but firmly.

"It's not the same," George told her. "And you could get a decent automobile. Tate's had that damn bus for years."

"His van is in great repair," Caren said defensively. "He does all the mechanical work and servicing himself, and he needs the space to transport his work. Besides, my car is only a year old."

George shook his head and sighed. "You don't know what's good for you both. I guess Tate will come to his senses one day, but then it might be too late."

"Too late for what?" Caren asked. "He's already a fairly well-known artist. He's made his mark."

"Artist," George sneered. "What kind of career is that for a man?"

"George!" Donna said sternly. "Do you want more potatoes?"

George took the hint and the subject was changed, but Caren continued to reflect on George's attitude. She had known he didn't approve of Tate's work, but this was the first time she'd ever actually heard him belittle it. Of course, Tate had always been present before, so George probably hadn't dared.

After dinner Caren helped Donna load the dishwasher and tidy up the kitchen while George retired to the study to work. The women were just finishing up when the phone rang.

"Can you get that, Caren?" Donna asked. "My hands are wet."

It was Tate. Caren took the call in the hallway, leaning against the wall instead of sitting at the ornate antique telephone table.

"Have you had dinner?" he asked.

"Have I! Your mother made a delicious roast pork with apple dressing. I also had lunch with Tanya and said hi to Ben. Did you eat yet?"

"I took a break for some cold chicken and salad, then went back to my painting. I've been working all day."

"Good for you," she applauded. "I'm missing you, Tate."

"I'm in knots for you," he said softly. "Do you know that?"

"No, I didn't know that," she said just as softly in reply. "Like to explain?"

As he described the things he'd like to do to her, she felt her body grow warm with longing. "I can't wait," she told him. "Save it for me, Tate."

"I will, honey. Have a good night. Can I speak to Mom?"

"Sure. Hold on," she said.

While Tate spoke to his mother, Caren wandered into the living room. She sat on the sofa by the window and gazed out over the garden. It was dark now, but lights illuminated the backyard and the snowy landscape that reminded her of the sand dunes by the lake below their house. How she missed Tate! A few hours away from him and already she couldn't wait to get back.

Donna came into the living room. "That was nice of Tate to phone. You must wonder why we never come up for a visit... Lord knows, I've suggested it to George often enough, but he insists he can't take the time from his business."

Caren inhaled sharply. Here was an opening for her to ask Donna about Tate and his father. "Don't you suppose the business is an excuse?" she asked her mother-in-law. "I mean, I've always sensed a certain tension between Tate and his father..."

Donna came over to the sofa and sat down next to Caren. "You're right about the tension," she said. "I think Tate's been trying to keep you out of it, but since you're obviously concerned, perhaps it would be best to speak of it openly. The relationship between George and Tate has always been a stormy one."

"From the little Tate has said, I've gathered there were some pretty big blow-ups in the past," Caren said. "But I thought that now, with Tate grown up, married, sticking by his choice of career and achieving recognition for his work...well, I thought they'd more or less buried the hatchet."

Donna made herself comfortable on the couch and crossed her legs. "They manage to be civil if they don't speak too much, but as soon as they start voicing ideas they get into an argument. George wanted all three of his sons in the business. When I had Tate seven years after Ron, he was overjoyed. George Ashley and Sons would prosper forever. When Tate began showing signs of being artistic, George was quite upset. He thinks every man should have lots of muscle and work at what he calls "a decent job.""

Caren smiled. "Tate has lots of muscle."

"Of course he does. In fact, he's in better physical shape than either Ron or Harry."

"He takes after his mother," Caren complimented.

"Why thank you." Donna paused for a moment, as if considering. "Actually we are very alike. I'm a bookworm and I love sewing and fancy embroidery; I even dabble a little in watercolors when I get around to it."

"So what's wrong with Tate being artistic? Frankly, I was a bit shocked by what George said at dinner about Tate's being a painter."

"He's never accepted it." Donna shook her head sadly. "I used to try to reason with him. After all, he had two other sons who were willing to be railroaded into the business. But not Tate—Tate wanted to go his own way, which he did.

"He left home at seventeen?" Caren said.

"He just walked out. He went to Toronto and phoned me later, saying I shouldn't worry. He had a terrible fight with his father before he left. George called him all sorts of hateful names. He even said"—Donna hesitated—"he even insinuated that Tate was not a real man. I was sick about the whole thing and furious with George. Eventually Tate broke the ice by visiting us, but he'd changed. He was harder, more determined to go after what he wanted. George should never have said what he did, especially to someone as sensitive as Tate."

"I had no idea," Caren said. She was upset that George would even think such a thing, let alone say it to Tate's face.

"George realizes now that he was wrong, but it's hard to say 'sorry' with a decade or more of damage between them."

"Poor Tate," Caren said.

"I'd like to think Tate didn't take it to heart, but I know he did. He loves his father. He wants George to respect his accomplishments. Personally, I admire Tate. He went out on a limb and achieved something. Tate knows I'm proud of him, but it's not enough; he needs George's support, too."

"Donna..." Caren paused to formulate her notion into words. "You don't suppose Tate thought the baby would prove anything to his father?"

Donna shrugged. "I'm really not sure if it bothered Tate to that extent or not. Let's hope it didn't. But why would you say that, Caren?"

"Oh, Donna." Caren stood up. "When I was pregnant, I had a feeling that something was troubling Tate. It was almost as if he were approaching a precipice in his life. I know that sounds dramatic, but that's how it was. Things started to go wrong in our marriage before I lost the baby. I began working harder and staying at the shop, hoping it would go away. I didn't want to see anything wrong. And then I lost the baby, and our relationship just fell apart. We had nothing until lately, and we've been trying hard, but I keep sensing that Tate's hiding something."

"And you think it's that he wanted the baby to prove to his father once and for all that he was a complete man?" Donna asked tightly.

Caren nodded.

"Oh, dear." Donna shook her head. "I'd hate to think that. Tate's sensitive, but he usually sees each side of a problem objectively."

"Except this problem," Caren interjected. She stared out the window into the dark. "How do I solve this one?"

"Well, it might not be true," Donna said. "You could talk to him about it and see what he says. Maybe it's just your imagination. I used to be very up and down when I was pregnant. And of course the first pregnancy is usually the most difficult."

"I know. I don't think I was accepting the full responsibility of the pregnancy, either." Caren sighed, "Oh, Donna, I love Tate so much."

"And he loves you," Donna assured her. "He dropped in just after he'd first met you and was making plans to settle in Russelton when he got the house. I'd seen him excited over women before, but never to such an extent. I had a feeling that there would be wedding bells. And when I met you, I knew for sure. I was very thankful he'd found someone who understood him so well."

"I just hope I can live up to your expectations," Caren said.

"You do." Donna stood up, saying, "Why don't I make a pot of tea, dear. It will calm us down. Then we'll have hot baths and a good night's sleep." She patted Caren's shoulder. "Don't worry too much. I think Tate's in for life with you."

"I hope you're right." Caren smiled, reassured by Donna's confidence in the marriage. After all, Tate's mother knew him better than anyone.

Donna returned her smile. "If not, I'll talk to him. That should set him straight."

After tea and the promised bath, Caren lay in the huge bed in the elaborately decorated guest room and stared at the patterned ceiling. On a white background, little flowers came swirling into the middle to meet in circles. The walls and carpet were rose colored and complemented the darker red drapes and bedspread. Caren had once joked to Tate that being in the room was like being in the middle of a paint pot.

Tate. She sighed, turning over on her side and pulling the covers around her, missing his lean, warm strength. But if she'd drawn the right conclusions from her talk with Donna, she had to face the fact that her husband had never fully confided in her. Tate had even, perhaps deliberately, tried to deceive her about the tension between himself and George. Didn't he trust her? And if not, how could there be love without trust?

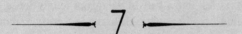

# 7

CAREN WOKE UP early in the morning and lazily enjoyed the large comfortable bed and softly decorated bedroom. She recalled how she and Tate had slept together in this same room, how they'd tried to make love without calling out. No matter what the circumstances, lovemaking always seemed to cement the bond between them. But had their love been too heavily based on sex, without an equal emotional intimacy?

She shuffled restlessly in the bed, remembering her conversation with Donna the evening before. Even though she'd spent half the night awake, she was no nearer a decision about what to do. She had rehearsed a few ways to approach her husband:

"Tate, I want to talk to you about your father."

Or maybe, "Tate, the baby, was it..."

No. Neither way seemed right. She kept thinking about Tate's angry reaction to her teasing remark about his dad the other day. Of course, she might be making a mountain out of a molehill. Tate might laugh his head off at her ideas, but somehow she didn't think so. Men were very sensitive about their roles.

With a sigh, Caren eased out of bed, glad to find the room warm, the carpet thick. The house in Russelton sometimes felt cold because of all the windows. Tate had sealed them as well as he could, but still there were drafts.

She went through to the adjoining pink bathroom, her nylon gown flowing around her ankles. Caren always felt like a lady of the manor in this house. She couldn't really see herself living in this style, though. It would suffocate her after a while. That's why she had always stayed in Russelton. She liked the outdoor life. She didn't have to drive to get to the country or the lake.

She stripped off her nightgown and stepped into the shower. Feeling invigorated after emerging from the warm spray, she dressed in a yellow cotton shirt and jeans. As she pulled on her socks, she remembered that her boots were downstairs by the front door. After brushing her hair, she dabbed on a bit of makeup and went down the wide, carpeted staircase.

George and Donna were in the living room, sharing breakfast. There was a delicious aroma of coffee in the house.

"Morning, Caren," George said cheerfully, standing up and straightening his gray suit. "Have a good night?"

"Very good, thank you." She smiled, taking a seat.

Donna, elegantly dressed as usual, even in the

morning, was wearing dark green slacks and a matching full-sleeved blouse. She poured Caren's coffee, then turned to her husband. "Are you off now, George?"

"Just going. Give my regards to Tate, Caren. We'd like to see him." He hugged his daughter-in-law briefly as he said good-bye.

Donna followed him to the front door. When she returned, she told Caren, "I'm trying to get him to retire. Hopefully, by spring he will. Harry's being coached to take over the company."

"What will George do when he retires?" Caren asked. It was hard to imagine Tate's father puttering around the house all day.

"Get under my feet no doubt." Donna laughed. "No, we plan to spend the winters down in Florida. We have a little condominium apartment there that we've been renting out. George likes to play golf, and I'm not averse to the game myself."

"I hope it works out," Caren said. "Is that why Harry's buying the new house?"

"Yes. Harry's such a go-getter. He likes to make an impression. Don't you want a more substantial breakfast than toast, Caren? I could make bacon and eggs, or pancakes."

"No, this is fine." Caren took a sip of freshly squeezed orange juice, then spread marmalade on a slice of toast. "I'd better be getting on home. I don't like to leave Tate too long."

"Things will work out for you," Donna said. "You want to be together. That's the main thing. Are you going to talk to him about what we discussed last night?"

"I'm not sure," Caren said. "I don't want to upset

him now that he's started working again."

"I'd play it by ear," Donna agreed. "If things are smooth now, it might be best to take everything gradually. I know you think George is brash and quite unlovable..." Donna put up her hand when Caren opened her mouth to protest. "He gives that impression sometimes, but it's all on the surface. George's capacity for tenderness and intimacy never fails to amaze me. He's worked hard in his business, but he's always had time for the kids and me. In fact, although he hides it well, he's a bit of an old softie really."

"Obviously you've had a good marriage."

"Oh, we've had our ups and downs, but we're still very close, and that's what counts. When I first met George, he was just getting started in the company. He was piled under with paper work and grudgingly decided that he had to have a secretary. Consequently, I was hired. I was petrified of him at first; but then he took me out to dinner a few times after I worked late. Our relationship grew from there. One night he bought me roses, and we went to bed. I don't think I've looked back from there."

Caren smiled, trying to picture a young George and Donna in love. Donna touched Caren's hand. "Don't ever let anyone tell you that sex isn't important in marriage. It's what binds two people who love each other into one. It keeps you close."

Caren nodded, dismissing her previous fears that she and Tate placed too much emphasis on their physical relationship. As Donna said, a good sex life was vital to true intimacy.

"You can work out your problems around it," Donna continued. "I know you're close to Tate. Harry and

Mary are pretty good, but I despair of Ron and Laura, although I never butt in unless I'm approached."

"I think you're fantastic," Caren told her mother-in-law warmly. "Tate's lucky."

"I think I'm lucky to have such a talented son." Donna smiled. "I enjoy his fame. Now don't worry too much, Caren. Things will work out."

Donna's comments gave Caren food for thought as she drove back to Russelton. It was another clear, bright day. The warmth from the sun melted the snow by the side of the road, and water ran in shiny rivers across the highway.

So much had happened to Caren over the past week or so that she felt almost swollen with feelings. Conflicting emotions drifted back and forth in her mind, but her love for Tate was strongly in the forefront. That was her anchor.

She reached home around lunchtime. Eager to see Tate, she left the car outside the garage and ran to the house. She met him rushing out to meet her, and they fell into each other's arms.

"I've missed you," he cried, lifting her high into the air.

"You were supposed to be working." She grinned, feeling dizzy from the height. "Let me down, Tate."

He dropped her to the ground and, as her stomach righted, he kissed her. "I did some work but I had to take a few hours off to sleep." After helping her remove her jacket and boots, he slung his arm across her shoulders and led her into the kitchen where lunch was set out on the table. "Sit down," he said.

He had heated up some lasagna he'd made and

frozen a while back, and he served it with a tossed salad. After pouring coffee, he took his place across from her.

Caren picked up her fork. She was sure this was leading up to something.

"Tanya phoned," he said without preamble. "She suggested a show in the spring—maybe April or May—and she wants to see my work. I understand they're coming up for the weekend." Tate stopped and twisted his coffee mug on the table. "Know anything about this?"

Caren shrugged. "She, uh, did mention something about how nice it would be for you to have another show, and I said, well yes, that's a good idea, why don't you call?"

He laughed. "You're not a very good liar, Caren darling. This one-man show of my paintings was all your idea, wasn't it?"

She blushed furiously. "I wanted to help, Tate."

"Okay, okay, I'm not complaining. It's probably what I need. I was thinking only the other day that if I had something definite to work toward, then maybe I'd be in better shape. But," he said, shrugging, "I can't do it."

She stared at him. "What do you mean, you can't do it?"

"I've only got one painting. I'd need at least another dozen for a show."

"You've done hundreds of paintings, Tate."

"Not in the last four months."

"But we're not talking about the last four months. We're talking about now. Besides, it's all arranged with Tanya. They're going to come and stay here overnight."

"I don't mind them staying here. It's the show I don't want."

Caren speared a piece of lettuce. "A show is just the incentive you need right now, Tate."

"So I promise a show and don't come across with the goods—is that what you want?" he demanded.

"You'll come across with the goods if I have to stand over you with a hammer to guarantee it," she retorted. "Tate, you've got to do this."

He raked his fingers through his hair, ruffling the black strands. "You don't understand, Caren. I can't turn my creativity on and off like a faucet."

His words stung her like a slap. "I do understand, Tate," she protested, then added ruefully, "Even you conceded that a few days ago, when you called me at the shop."

A look of dismay came into his vivid blue eyes. "Now you're angry, and that's the last thing I wanted."

"Not angry, Tate. Hurt." She knew how he hated confrontations and quarrels, but she had to risk it: Tate needed this show.

"Oh, Caren . . ." He made a movement to rise from his chair, but she shook her head.

"No, Tate, we have to talk about it." They stared at each other across the kitchen table, lunch forgotten.

"All right," he acquiesced. "Let's talk."

Gratefully, she reached for his hand and gave it a warm squeeze. "Tate, I do realize the show puts a certain pressure on you to produce. But you painted *Breakaway* with lightning speed and immediately started in on the next canvas. I know your rhythms. You paint a series at a time, and it's always the first painting of the series that's the toughest."

"Exactly," he said. "I'll need more than one series

to mount an exhibition. What if I get blocked again?"

"I don't think you will. Once your momentum gets under way, you always paint several series at a stretch. Why should this time be any different? Look, Tate, I can see that Tanya's phone call has thrown you into something of a panic, but I'm sure that's only a temporary reaction. You know how much having your work exhibited means to you. Ultimately the show will give you new impetus. I'm sure of that—I believe in you, darling."

As he listened to his wife's impassioned declaration of faith, Tate felt his tense muscles relax. Caren was right—despite the anxiety, a feeling of excitement was already stirring inside him at the thought of a one-man show. He admitted to himself that part of his resistance came from a fear that he had to be successful in order to keep Caren's love. He was so conscious of his failure to paint these past months, that at first he'd thought she'd engineered the show only because she needed assurance that she was married to a somebody.

But now, seeing the love and concern that radiated from Caren's every feature, he realized he'd wronged her. All Caren's maneuvering had been for *his* sake. She'd been trying to restore his confidence in himself, trying to remind him that there were people out there clamoring to see Tate Ashley's latest work. She *did* believe in him, and with a choked-up feeling he made a silent vow to be worthy of that belief.

"I love you, Caren," he said huskily. "I love you so much."

"I love you, too, Tate. I don't want us to break up."

"We won't," he said forcefully. "Never."

She blinked back tears. "Will you do the show?"

"The idea still scares me a little, but the excitement's mounting too," he said. "Anyway, I'll at least talk to Tanya about it."

She couldn't hope for any more than that, and she returned to her lunch. "This is good."

"I know you never eat breakfast."

"I did have toast this morning. By the way, your mom sends her love. And your dad sends his."

"Does he?" Tate sounded skeptical.

It was her cue to plunge right in with her newfound discovery, but she couldn't do it. Something kept her tongue-tied. Probably the delicacy of the subject and the fact that it wasn't really the right moment, what with all his tension over the art show. There were a multitude of reasons, and she didn't want to strain their relationship any more than necessary.

So Caren limited her lunchtime conversation to describing the drive down to London, the meal with Tanya, and her evening with his parents.

"How did my dad seem?" he asked with what Caren thought was studied casualness.

"I really only saw him briefly over dinner and breakfast," she said. "Apparently he's on the verge of retiring."

"At last," Tate said. "Mother's wanted that for years. Is Harry taking over?"

"Of course. He's already slotting himself in. He's buying a three-hundred-thousand-dollar house with two swimming pools."

"Good Lord!" Tate laughed. "It's hard to believe they're my flesh and blood."

"They are, though," Caren said. "You have to face up to it, Tate."

"Oh, I've always faced it," he replied. "But some-times I just find it incredible. When I was a kid, my father used to take me along to building sites. He always drove a huge Lincoln then, before gas prices went up. He'd walk me around, showing me brick-layers and concrete pourers. He'd say, 'Son, one day you'll be doing that. You have to have on-the-job training before you can take over the company.'"

"And what did you say?" Caren asked, a picture of George, with Tate as a child clearly in her mind.

"'No way, Dad.'"

"And then?"

"He'd get red in the face and say, 'Son, soon you'll be a man. You'll have a wife one day and you'll have to support her.'"

Caren began to titter, because Tate was sounding just like his father. "And then what?"

"I'd say, 'My wife will probably have to support me.'"

"Oh, no." Caren stifled her laughter.

"He'd go into a rage then. We'd ride home with him, blustering and me defiant, and my mother would scold both of us. It's funny now in retrospect, but it wasn't so funny at the time." Tate glanced down at the table and sighed. "He never gave up, though. At meals he would always dominate the conversation. Harry and Ron used to drive me up the wall, the way they took it all. He'd tell us stories of how hard he had worked. How he started as a one-man builder doing all the labor himself, and then on and on. I admired his perserverance, but I had to go my own way. I saw life from a very different perspective."

"Your mother told me that he's quite soft really," Caren said tentatively.

"He is. He protects himself, that's all. Still, he really does believe some of those things he says. Don't underestimate him."

"I've always been a little scared of him," Caren admitted.

"He wants people to fear him. Ron and Harry are still terrified."

"And you?" Caren asked, knowing she was treading on delicate ground.

"I regret that we can't be friends because of his prejudices," Tate said. "Instead, we have to relate on a strictly superficial level to keep the peace. Oh, well." He finished his salad and pushed his plate aside. "So, how was my mother?"

"As terrific as ever. She's hoping to get your father to Florida for the winters if he retires."

"Good luck to her." He grinned and got to his feet. "Come on, let's clean up. I've got something to show you."

He had started a second painting overnight, and its relationship to the first one was clear. This time the child had been caught in the grasping hands. "Is it going to be a long series?" she asked.

"I think so. Do you like them?"

"Very much. You've always shied away from painting people before, but you're really good at it. This could open up a whole new direction for you."

"Or I could come to a dead end," he said pessimistically.

"Tate," she admonished, "you're just putting obstacles in the way. I showed Tanya a photograph of *Breakaway,* and she was very impressed."

He shook his head at her. "I can't trust you to go anywhere, can I?"

"Going to keep me in line?" she asked coyly, suddenly feeling a strong desire to get close to him, to reassure herself that he was hers.

His blue eyes turned warm. "Do you want to be kept in line?"

"Please," she breathed, and stepped closer to him.

He took her into his arms, and she clung to him tightly. He buried his mouth in her hair. "Why do you always smell so sweet? You've got beautiful hair, lady." He kissed her before he picked her up in his arms. "Now I've got something else to show you."

"Ooh, tell me," she said laughingly.

"I said *show* you," he reprimanded. "I've been saving it all night."

"You bad man." She nuzzled his neck with her mouth, loving the taste of him.

"How do you know it's that?" He placed her on the bed and lay down on top of her.

She stretched beneath him, fitting her curves to his hard virility. "It had better be that."

He opened her blouse and pressed his palm over her breasts. He lifted the fullness and kissed each one. Then he pulled the zipper on her jeans, his hands wandering to the edge of her lace panties. "It's that," he said breathlessly.

"I can feel it." She gave his hand access to stroke her quivering flesh as she unbuttoned his shirt and ran her hands down over his chest hair. She slipped his shirt down one shoulder and sensuously licked his salty skin. "I want you."

"I more than want you," he groaned, his hands urgent on her body. "I'm on fire for you, angel."

The deep passion seemed to spring from nowhere.

They were naked, joined, pushing upward into shattering union.

"Where does it come from?" Caren asked, tears sliding down her cheeks when it was over. Tate was still kissing her body, his mouth tender.

"I don't know. It's like a mystery—inexplicable but wonderful."

She ruffled his hair as he finally relaxed against her breasts. "I could stay here forever with you."

"Then don't move," he whispered. "This is the best place I've ever been."

Just as Caren smiled contentedly and closed her eyes, she realized that once again she had let slide the perfect opportunity to discuss his father.

# 8

THE WEEK FLEW by with Tate painting up a storm. Every evening, Caren returned from the shop to find him still engrossed at his easel. He hardly seemed aware of her presence as she stood behind him and watched the *Breakaway* series take shape, smiling to herself at the sight of her husband as a whirling dervish of energy and ambition. But she was careful not to let Tate exhaust himself, determinedly coaxing him away from his canvas each night to share the simple meals she had again begun preparing for their dinner.

"You know, Caren, I think your cooking has definitely improved," he complimented her Thursday night over a meal of broiled lamb chops with mint jelly, a casserole of string beans and mushrooms, with baked stuffed clams as an appetizer.

"Maybe you're just too absorbed in your painting to really taste what you're eating," she teased.

"No," he said seriously. "The lamb's just right—crisp on the outside and tender on the inside—and the casserole is superb. The stuffed clams were very tasty, too."

"I bought them ready-made at the deli and just heated them up," she confessed. "And even a culinary moron can broil lamb chops."

He gave her a searching look. "Are you just being modest, or do you resent having to do the cooking?"

"Not at all!" she exclaimed. "It's high time I started pulling my weight around this house again, Tate. It's just that I know I don't have your knack for gourmet cooking. Though I am rather proud of the string-bean casserole. I mean, it's the first really creative dish I've ever tried that's come out right."

"See? Practice makes perfect."

"I think it's a question of patience. I used to think cooking was sort of a waste of time. I didn't want to put a whole lot of energy into something so ephemeral. The shop was my 'real' life, you know? But lately I haven't been getting such a charge out of Caren's Crafts."

"No?" Tate lifted a concerned eyebrow.

"Oh, I still enjoy the creative end of it," she told him. "I'm doing another of those macramé-and-pottery hangings. But the business part has become pretty ho-hum for me, and I find myself delegating more and more of it to David."

"I see. But what's that got to do with your changed attitude toward cooking?"

"Maybe my values are changing. I mean, I used to see business as solid, satisfying—now I'm getting bored with it. On the other hand, cooking is like a new horizon for me, and I realize that even if a meal doesn't endure, it still provides a qualitative satisfaction."

"I've always felt that way," he said. "You know that Pillsbury motto; 'Nothin' says lovin' like something from the oven'? Well, it's corny but true. To me, a meal is a kind of offering to the senses."

"Exactly," she agreed. "I wonder why I never saw it that way before. Maybe"—she hesitated—"maybe I've been taking an attitude like your father's, Tate. Rigidly evaluating things according to a preconceived standard. I mean, I thought that since a meal doesn't last it therefore doesn't matter. Just as your father thinks art has no 'useful' purpose, and therefore has no legitimacy."

Tate's smile had faded at her mention of his father. "Caren," he said, his face closed. "I don't know what you're getting at, but I've never seen the slightest resemblance between you and my father. Look, I'm not in the mood for discussing him tonight. Let's forget him—let's forget everything except you and me, okay?"

Her instinct told her not to push it, but rather to lighten the tension between them. "Okay," she said, her eyes gleaming mischievously. "I guess that means to forget the chocolate mousse I whipped up for dessert, right? Too bad. I couldn't resist a taste, and it's so rich, so delectable..."

He caught her mood and grinned. "Unfair, Caren. You know my weakness for chocolate desserts."

"Oh, but we have to forget it," she said with exaggerated virtue.

"Lady, we'll forget it after we've eaten it," he

growled. "Now bring it here before I have a choco-
holic seizure and go eat it all myself."

"Oh, no, you don't! I get to eat the fruit of my
labors," she said, laughing.

A devilish gleam sparked his eyes. "I'll give you
till the count of three."

She made it to the refrigerator by the count of two,
but he was right behind her. Like children, they scooped
the mousse from the one bowl with two spoons. And
like lovers, they licked the chocolate from each other's
fingers, whetting an appetite that could only be satis-
ifed in the bedroom.

Caren took Friday off, and she and Tate spent the
morning tidying up the spare bedroom. Tanya and
Ben's silver-gray BMW pulled into the driveway in
the middle of the afternoon. Tanya had two large black
suitcases, while Ben had a small tan leather bag.

"How long do you think you're staying?" Tate asked
Tanya, picking up the cases after all the hugs and
kisses were over.

"Maybe I'm planning on longer than the weekend."
Tanya smiled. "It's great to get away from the city
for a while. We really appreciate this."

"It's great to have you," Tate said warmly. "How's
it going, Ben?"

"In the best way possible," Ben said. "You two
look happy."

"We are," Caren acknowledged. "Come on in; it's
freezing."

As usual, Tanya came loaded with gifts: homemade
chocolate-chip cookies (Tate's favorite) and brownies.
There was a box of herbal tea for Caren and some
chocolate mints.

"Are you trying to fatten us up?" Caren laughed. "Thanks though, Tanya. We've both been on a chocolate binge, and you've given us an excuse to continue indulging ourselves."

Tanya and Ben loved their bedroom, and they loved the house. Caren had roast turkey and all the trimmings in the oven, but before their meal they dressed warmly and trudged down the hillside to the snowy beach. There was ice on the edge of the lake, but Tate managed to find some clear space to skim some stones.

"You're good at that, Tate," Tanya said, stuffing her hands in the pockets of her fur jacket. "We should have a contest sometime."

Tate put his gloves back on. "Then let's make it summer. My fingers are freezing."

"Can you swim here in the summer?" Ben asked Caren.

"Oh, sure." She nodded. "It's terrific. Our own private beach."

"We'll come back in the summer," Tanya promised. "After Tate's given us a sell-out show and we can afford the gas."

Tate ruffled her auburn curls. "Now I have to live up to my reputation."

"You'd better, Tate Ashley. I'm depending on you for this one."

Caren gave Tate a sideways glance, but she couldn't read his expression.

After dinner, Caren served coffee by a roaring fire and they all sat in the dark, lounging around on the cushions. Caren lay with her head in Tate's lap while Tanya leaned into Ben. The talk was sporadic but serious, and Tate opened up in the company of Tanya and Ben.

At midnight when Caren put on more coffee and served cheese and crackers, they began to discuss art. The conversation went on in quite a heated manner until almost three in the morning, at which time Caren, though interested, knew she had to go to sleep. They finally all stumbled up to bed.

"I'm sleeping late tomorrow morning," Tanya promised.

"And then she'll take at least an hour in the bathroom," Ben said. "So be warned."

"Breakfast is at nine-thirty," Tate caroled. "And I'm cooking."

"Then we're going walking," Caren added. "No sleeping late for this crowd."

In bed, Caren rolled into Tate's arms. "Hug me tight, darling."

"I'm going to do more than that," he told her softly, planting little kisses over her earlobe.

"With guests in the house?"

He laughed. "Some things can't be kept down . . ."

In the morning they went for a long walk, taking the trails through the woods above the lake. Melting snow dripped from the sun-warmed trees, and the air was fresh and crisp. Below them, the lake was a grayish blue reflecting the wintry sky.

Both couples held hands and made zany jokes as they strolled through the countryside. Caren felt more exhilarated than she had in months. She felt like standing in the middle of a field and yodeling with joy.

When they returned to the house, they ate a lunch of ham sandwiches and hot chocolate. Tanya, Ben, and Tate got down to the business of talking about Tate's work. Caren didn't want to be a part of the discussion, afraid that for all his recent activity Tate might still panic and back out of the show. So she cleaned up the kitchen and prepared the evening meal. It was only cold cuts—turkey, pressed ham and some simple salads—but Caren wanted it right. She was entertaining Tate's business associates, after all.

Ben suggested that they have a romantic evening, so both women dressed up for dinner. Tanya wore a long black wool dress that emphasized her upswept auburn curls and gave her skin an added glow. Caren put on a silky hunter-green jumpsuit that hugged her curves and accented her beautiful emerald eyes. She brushed her hair until it shone and tied it back with a green satin ribbon. Finally, she sprayed on an exotic perfume Donna had given her at Christmas and slipped her feet into backless suede shoes.

"Wow!" Ben exclaimed when he saw her. "Tate and Tanya, did I hear you say you were going out?"

"Not on your life." Tate slipped his arm around Caren and kissed her cheek. "You look lovely."

She glanced sideways at his black cords and black silk shirt. "You look lovely, too," she whispered.

For some reason, Tate's body tensed at her comment. What have I done? Caren thought, but Tate was already leading everyone to the table for dinner.

Throughout the meal, Caren noticed that Tate seemed slightly on edge. It was probably so subtle that Ben and Tanya would miss it, but Caren had grown attuned to her husband's every mood. She recalled her conversation with Donna, and wished she had kept her mouth shut now. She had only meant, "You look lovely, too," as a joke, not as a slight against his masculinity but suddenly she remembered her other joke about his "daddy" and his negative reaction then. Maybe her theory about Tate's motives for wanting the baby were right. She felt a hard shaft of anger toward George Ashley for all the damage he had wrought with his careless words.

She looked at Tate, who was smiling at one of Ben's anecdotes. She didn't think she would ever have the courage to broach the subject with him.

After dinner, they closed the door on the dishes and returned to the living room. Tate put an album on the stereo and a haunting saxophone sounded through the room, giving the impression that they were in a smoky jazz club. It was a clear night, and stars twinkled through the skylights. Determined to reassure Tate, Caren slipped her arms around his neck and gave him a kiss.

He hugged her, sliding his hands over her silky back. So she had noticed his discomposure. He hated to think that his father could intrude on his relationship with Caren.

Tanya turned two spotlights on so they illuminated Tate's paintings and gazed at his work through narrowed eyes.

"Oh, this stuff is really good, Tate. I love the third one you're working on. The baby theme really comes through."

Caren moved closer into the little tableau that Tate, Tanya, and Ben made in the light, and studied Tate's third *Breakaway* painting. She saw a child in a protected environment, while above, as though on a street, people's feet and legs were moving, trampling. It had the same eerie quality that made the other two so interesting. Her hand touched her stomach as if to protect something, and when she realized there wasn't anything to protect, she dropped her hand and took a step backward on her high heels.

Tate glanced at her, and she smiled. This was his moment. Tanya and Ben were so enthusiastic about his work that he couldn't help but be encouraged.

"You're right on track again, Tate," Tanya said. "Don't back out on me now."

"I won't," Tate told her. "But it's delicate."

Ben patted his shoulder. "You'll do fine, Tate."

Caren reached for Tate's fingers and squeezed tightly. "So let's celebrate. Why don't you put something lively on the stereo, Tate? And Ben, I know you'd love another beer."

Ben laughed. "How did you guess? We'll have a toast to Tate. To a successful show."

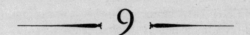

# 9

THE NEXT MORNING, Caren, Tate, and Ben were in the kitchen talking over toast and coffee when Tanya came floating down in a nearly see-through black negligee.

She yawned and took a seat next to her husband. "Pardon my dress."

"What there is of it," Tate commented.

Tanya laughed. "I'm an old woman, Tate."

"Don't bet on it." Ben leered at his wife.

Caren looked at Tanya. "Want some coffee?"

Tanya's mouth turned down at the edges. "I'm not sure."

"Toast?" Tate offered.

Tanya turned pale and stood up. "Excuse me . . ."

Ben followed Tanya's hurried exit out of the kitchen

while Tate and Caren exchanged glances.

"She probably ate too much last night," Tate said.

"Maybe," Caren agreed, but suddenly her own toast and coffee didn't seem very appetizing. She was reminded of the morning sickness she'd suffered when she was pregnant, and she felt a strange longing course through her.

Seeing her set features, Tate asked, "Anything wrong?"

Caren shook her head just as Ben and Tanya walked back into the kitchen. Tanya was now dressed in jeans with a black cotton shirt hanging outside. They sat down at the table, Tanya still pale.

They both looked as if they had something to say, and Caren knew instinctively what it was before Ben slid his arm around his wife's shoulders.

"I know we must seem like old fogies to you," he said. "But Tanya's pregnant."

Tanya's smile was quavery. "We're taking a risk, you know. I'm older than the average mother, of course. But these days, what with amniocentesis and all . . . well, the doctor says I'm healthy enough."

"Despite this," Ben said, pointing to his curly gray hair and beard, "I'm not as old as I look. I think I can handle fatherhood."

"I know you can." Tanya moved closer to him. "You handle husbandhood pretty well."

Tate glanced at Caren. She hadn't said a word throughout this interchange. Her face was pale, and he felt sorry for her as he thought about her dreams of having a family, her agony over the baby she'd lost. He'd had his dreams as well, but they were now coming out in his work, almost unwillingly. He felt he should say something to Ben and Tanya.

"Congratulations. That's great, you two."

"You don't think we're too old?" Tanya asked.

"My parents were older, and I never had a problem," Caren contributed. To her own ears her voice sounded as if it were coming from a long way off. She didn't know what was wrong with her. Usually she was warm and exuberant over others' good news, but she couldn't deny she was jealous of Tanya's pregnancy. She remembered making the same announcement not too long ago, giddy with pleasure and pride.

Ben grinned. "And look at Caren. She's beautiful."

Caren forced a smile. "Thanks. I'm sure everything will go well." She stood up hurriedly. "Look, Tanya, why don't you rest for a while? Ben and Tate can go for a walk in the sunshine while I clean up in here."

As if sensing her need to be alone, they all did as she suggested.

Tate walked with Ben across the crisp snow. He had always thought of Ben as a large man, but now he saw that he topped his older friend by an inch or two. Tate had come to like Ben a lot over the years. Tanya's husband was sensitive and perceptive, the kind of man Tate's father could never understand.

"We didn't intend to break our news that way," Ben said. "I hope we haven't upset Caren."

"Don't worry about it," Tate reassured him. "Caren's miscarriage was a shock to both of us, but I think we're out of the woods now."

"Tanya mentioned that Caren told her it was really rough."

Tate sighed. "We were unprepared emotionally, but I think we're coping now."

"I understand." Ben nodded. "I'm trying to prepare myself. Tanya and I have a nice, stable relationship, and I'm a little worried that a baby might disrupt it. I mean, part of me is ecstatic, but the other part worries about the changes in our lifestyle. Four o'clock feedings, colic, and all that. To tell the truth, Tate, I feel a bit scared. Overwhelmed."

Tate nodded sympathetically. "Still, I have to admit I envy you," he said wistfully.

Ben's gaze was compassionate. "I know losing the baby was a trauma for both you and Caren. But didn't the doctor say you could still have other children?"

"Yes," Tate replied. "Caren isn't ready yet, though."

"Just give her time. She'll get over this."

Tate nodded, but he was troubled. He'd thought Caren had worked through her bereavement over the miscarriage, but her reaction to Tanya's news made him wonder. He wanted so badly to try for another child, but he knew that this time the suggestion would have to come from Caren.

They returned to the house and packed the suitcases in the car. Tate noticed that Caren's cheerfulness seemed forced and very brittle, but he didn't think the others recognized her mood, and if they did they were tactful enough not to mention it.

He placed a blanket over Tanya's lap as she snuggled into the front seat. "Have to keep that little one warm."

Tanya touched his hand and said, "Thanks for having us. I'm glad you're doing the show."

"I'm glad, too," he said.

He closed the car door and stood back with Caren. He could feel her tension, and he ached for her pain.

They both waved good-bye as the car disappeared down the driveway.

Caren turned and went into the house, relieved that she could now let go of her emotions. Tanya was pregnant—but no, it wasn't really that news that bothered her. It was just that it revived all her feelings about having a baby. All the pain and memories flooded back, and she realized that the sense of loss was still very strong. She'd thought her talk with Tate about the miscarriage had purged those deep feelings of grief, but now they welled up inside her as strong as ever.

Tears streaming from her eyes, she ran up the stairs and into the bedroom. She closed the door behind her, her breath coming in gulps. She didn't want Tate to see her like this, but she couldn't stop the agony. She threw herself on the bed and buried her face in the pillow, trying not to cry; but eventually her restraint burst and the pillow muffled her sobs. She didn't even hear the door open.

Tate sat down beside her and stroked her hair, trying to soothe her. She was holding herself tight to keep from trembling.

"Don't," he whispered. "Don't do this to yourself."

"The baby," she sobbed. "I thought I was recovered, but as soon as Tanya mentioned being pregnant, it all came back like a flash flood."

Tate's fingers massaged the back of her neck, easing the tension in the knotted muscles there. "You know, Caren," he said softly, "I just remembered something that happened when I was thirteen. My mom's mother had died the year before, and Mom had taken it pretty hard. But as the months passed, she became her old cheerful self again. Then, suddenly, one day as we were all sitting around looking through some family picture albums, she came across a photo of her mother as a young woman and just started crying as if her heart would break."

"She did?" Caren found it hard to picture the usually ebullient Donna in tears.

"Uh-huh. My brothers and I were totally stunned—in fact, the sight of Mom crying pretty well unnerved me. But my father went over to her, and without saying a word, he just began to rub her neck the way I'm doing to you now. After a few minutes, the tears stopped as abruptly as they'd come. I have to admit I was surprised by Dad's sensitivity. I can still see that scene so vividly in my mind: Mom's grief, my father's tenderness. And then it was as if she suddenly remembered us boys, and she felt she had to apologize. She said something like you did just now—'I thought I was over it, but the picture brought back all the pain.'"

"You mean, maybe my reaction was a natural one and I'm not grieving inordinately over the baby? It's strange, because lately I hadn't thought so much about losing it."

"That could be the explanation. You were caught unawares."

She turned to look at him, and he cradled her in his arms. "I guess you're right, Tate," she said slowly. "I remember after my father died, I used to have this recurring dream that he was still alive. Even when I hadn't been consciously thinking of him for a while, the dream would suddenly come back. I thought of it as the resurrection dream. I told my mother about it, and she said maybe that was my way of dealing with a lot of emotions I couldn't face openly. Maybe I had to bring back my father through that dream and resolve some loose ends in our relationship before I could really let him go."

Tate nodded. "Did you have a similar experience when your mom died?"

She shook her head. "No. I was older then, and I guess more able to deal with my feelings on a conscious level."

"And that's how you're dealing with your feelings about the baby, too," he said, rocking her gently in his arms. "You have the advantage over me there, Caren. It's hard for me to acknowledge my emotions sometimes. I tend to cope with them subconsciously, in my painting."

"I wondered if you weren't doing that in *Breakaway*," she suggested. "Dealing with feelings about your own childhood, and also about... our baby."

"Most likely I was, although I don't like to analyze the personal element in my work," he said. "You know, angel, it's strange, but somehow your tears a moment ago released something inside of me. First I felt your pain, and then it was my own pain surfacing, too." He placed his cheek next to hers, and for a moment they just rested together, sharing a time of silent closeness.

Caren was the first to speak. "Tate, one of the things that upset me about my response to Tanya's being pregnant was that I know how badly you'd like to try to have another baby. But I'm still afraid, and—"

He stopped her with a light kiss on the lips. "It's all right, Caren. There's no rush. Your happiness is more important to me than all the babies in the world."

"But the baby would have been a fulfillment of our love."

"There are many ways to fulfill our love. Do you remember when we first met I said that if I were a portrait painter I'd want to paint you? Well, now that I've been using human forms in *Breakaway*, the idea of painting you has begun to haunt me again. I thought of a series—my first vision of you by the lake, that night we made love by the fire, you as a bride, you working on your pottery at Caren's Crafts..."

"Oh, Tate! I'm so moved, darling." Tears sprang to her eyes again, but this time they were tears of joy.

"I even have a name for the series—*Portraits of My Love*."

Words failed her, and she could only try to express the depth of her emotion with a long kiss.

Tate's answering kiss conveyed both tenderness and passion. With loving fingers, he wiped the tears from her cheeks.

"It's so crazy," she murmured. "A few moments ago I felt so terrible, and now I feel so happy."

"You won't mind posing for the series?" he asked her anxiously. "I mean, I can use photographs and imagination—you know my work isn't all that representational anyway. I don't want to tire you out, but it would help if you could model for me a little in the evenings. I'll start making dinner again, so you can rest up then."

"I'd love to pose for you, Tate," she said. "And I don't mind sharing the cooking. Maybe we could even prepare some meals together. You could teach me how to make a few of the fancier dishes."

"I'd enjoy that," he said. "But I don't want you to get exhausted after a whole day at the shop."

"I can leave the shop a little earlier on the days you want me to pose," she offered. "You still have a few more paintings in the *Breakaway* series first, though, don't you?"

"Yes. Actually, I wasn't going to say anything about painting you until I'd finished that series. But this seemed to be the time."

"Yes, I'm glad you told me now. It really helped lift my spirits. But, Tate, I don't want you to feel you have to pamper me while I'm posing for you. It's not such hard work, I'm sure, and I have a strong constitution."

He grinned. "Famous last words. You should talk to a professional model about how exhausting it can be to remain perfectly passive for an hour. Besides, I enjoy pampering you a bit. In fact, I think you could use a little pampering right now. Why don't I make you a cup of that herbal tea Tanya brought?"

"Tea and sympathy?" she teased, smiling. "Why not!

"Caren felt strangely tranquil the next morning when she went in to work. David was quiet and thoughtful as he fashioned an intricate pot on his wheel, and Caren left him to it by perching on a stool behind the counter and doing some potting herself.

But to her surprise, once she had worked the air holes out of the clay, instead of throwing it on her potter's wheel to make a mug, she began sculpting it with her hands. As if of its own volition, the clay began to take shape as the bust of a young boy.

"It's our son, isn't it, Caren?"

Though Tate spoke softly, Caren was startled by the sound of his voice behind her. She hadn't heard him come into the shop. She turned around, and her heart caught at the sight of his large frame in his navy parka and jeans. She gazed in silence at the familiar handsome face for a moment. Then she remembered his question.

"Is it?" Taking Tate's hand, she turned back to the bust and examined it. "I suppose it is. Something must have taken root in me during our talk yesterday. The idea of art as therapy—although I had no idea what I was doing until this sort of spontaneously created itself beneath my fingers."

"I like it very much, Caren."

"You should," she teased with a nervous laugh. "I mean, given that it's a little replica of you!"

"That's not what I meant."

"I know. I have to admit I'm proud of it," she said. "I'm really kind of amazed that I could do anything so creative, though."

"The wall hanging you made was creative," he pointed out.

"True. I told you that came from your influence on me—and this did, too."

He took her in his arms and held her close. "I love you, Caren," he breathed against her ear.

"Tate, Tate . . . my darling Tate," she murmured. But suddenly she drew back to look at him. "Say, how come you're here in the middle of the morning? Nothing's wrong, is it?"

"Not a thing," he replied cheerfully. "And it's really not the middle of the morning—more like early afternoon. I came by to ask you out to lunch. I thought we might go up to the hotel."

"Sounds lovely," she said. "Let me just get my jacket and ask David to look after the store while I'm gone. I'm sure he won't mind."

"He'd better not," Tate teased as he released her.

"I'll just be a sec," she promised, moving toward the studio.

It was a sunny day with a hint of spring in the air even though there was still a lot of crisp snow on the ground. Tate took her hand as they walked to where he'd parked the van. It reminded her of other times, especially when they'd been going together before they were married. He would take her out for lunch every day. Sometimes down to the beach with a picnic, sometimes to a restaurant. Then he'd pick her up when the shop closed and they would go to his house and fall onto his bed . . . So much had happened since then. Caren sighed. She was no longer so young, or so innocent.

She climbed into the van, pushing her hood from her head. Her hair tumbled in a brilliant mass around her shoulders, picking up the glints of sunshine. Tate put out his hand to touch the bright strands. His fingers played with it soothingly as he drove through the town.

They reached the hotel, parked, and walked inside. They took window seats overlooking the lake, which sparkled gray-blue in the midday sunshine. They both ordered beef stew and Caesar salads.

"I see a hard morning's work has given you a healthy appetite," Tate remarked as they ate.

"I'm just taking the opportunity of having a decent lunch for a change," she said, smiling. "Usually I just grab a cheese sandwich."

"Now that you're learning to cook yourself, you'll find you become more discriminating about what you eat," he predicted.

"Maybe," she conceded. "This stew is certainly delicious."

Over coffee they chatted about the weekend and Tanya and Ben's response to Tate's work.

"I thought they seemed knocked out," he said cautiously. "What did you think?"

"They definitely liked it. I can tell with Tanya. She gets that vague air when she doesn't really like something. She's pretty honest."

"I hope they're honest. I wouldn't like to think that I was selling them short."

"Hardly. That's great stuff, Tate. Just keep it up."

He grinned. "I need you for my morale, you know."

"I need you as well. It was such a wonderful surprise when you walked into the store today."

"I came as the cheering-up committee of one," he said. "You've done it so often for me."

"It evens out," she told him. "We're in this together, Ashley."

He reached across the table to take her hand. His fingers rubbed absently at her wedding band. "By the way, I almost forgot. Grace Stark called this morning to ask if we would attend one of the ski club socials. I said we would. I think we should get out and about again."

Caren nodded. "Lord, yes. She mentioned that to me weeks ago, and I forgot to tell you. When is it?"

"Two weeks from Saturday. We have to bring a dish of hot food. Maybe that could be our first jointly prepared casserole."

"Sounds good. We'll have to get the skis out."

"I'll do that. You know, Caren, I think this outing will be fun."

"We could both use a little old-fashioned fun."

Caren sighed and then checked her watch. "I'd better get going. David must be starved by now."

Tate drove her back downtown and walked her to the shop. David was indeed looking hungry, and he went off to pick up his lunch while Tate kissed Caren good-bye in the back studio.

"I guess we haven't got time for dessert?" he said between kisses.

"David will be back in a minute." Caren laughed. "You're insatiable, Ashley."

"It's always been one of my most basic hungers."

"So I've noticed." She writhed against him to give him something to think about all afternoon, then stepped back. "Now go away; you disturb my peace of mind."

He grinned and finally left with another wave through the window.

Caren went back to work feeling happy and re-freshed.

Over the next week, business in the shop became quite brisk, as local residents, weary of winter, began arriving in town. Caren was busy getting a supply of mugs and pots ready for sale in the shop, but she managed to finish the bust of the child as well as begin work on another macramé-and-pottery wall hanging. Tate completed a fourth painting in the *Breakway* series, and started the fifth and final painting of the group. Caren had never seen his energy level so high. He insisted on taking over the cooking again, too, pointing out that she was having a hectic time in the shop and would need to rest up to pose for him. Caren didn't protest; for a change she was only too grateful for the chance to relax after work and then sit down with Tate to one of his gourmet dinners.

On Friday she had a particularly tiring day and went home feeling exhausted.

She slipped her car into the garage beside the van and walked into the house. It was very dark. Tate wasn't working in his studio, although Caren could smell the delicious aroma of something cooking.

She threw down her purse and peeled off her jacket, gloves, and boots.

"Tate," she called and then stopped. He'd set the little round table in the corner of the room for two. There were red placemats on the wooden surface and two red candles flickering in the center. Sparkling wineglasses held red paper napkins.

Caren smiled to herself. What was all this about? Instead of going into the kitchen, she climbed the stairs. She stripped off her jeans and shirt and took a quick shower. Then she put on a long purple dress of heavy cotton. It had a low slit over her breasts fastened by black velvet loops. She brushed her hair and repaired her makeup. Barefoot, she slipped downstairs and poked her head around the kitchen door. The room was bathed in the low light over the stove. Tate was cooking something there.

"Do I sense a romantic setting?" she said huskily.

He turned and smiled as he saw her dress. "Ah, good, you got the hint." He was wearing black velvet pants and a black silk shirt.

"I'm glad I did. Look at my sexy husband." She moved up behind him and slipped her arms around his waist. "You feel so good."

"So do you."

She leaned her cheek against his broad back, and asked, "What's the occasion?"

"Three-and-a-half years married and I've finished my fifth painting. How about a day of rest tomorrow and then Sunday you start to pose for me?"

"Sounds fine." She kissed his back. "What's that wonderful smell?"

"It's Chinese beef. I thought I'd get some use out of the wok Mom gave us."

"I can't wait to taste it. Did anyone ever tell you that you're the best husband in the world?"

"Not recently, but if you keep mauling me like that you might not get supper until later."

"What's for dessert?"

"You and me in front of the fire," he said softly.

"Sounds delicious. I'm starved." She moved away from him and leaned against the counter to watch.

Tate returned her gaze. "Got anything on under the dress?"

"Black silk panties with red hearts. Got anything on under those black velvet pants?"

He shook his head.

"Quick-Draw McGraw." She laughed.

But over dinner she sobered as she toasted her husband across the candlelit table. "We're making it, Tate," she said softly.

"If not now, we will be later." He grinned.

Caren smiled. "Aren't you ever serious?"

"We've been serious long enough," he said. "Let's start enjoying life."

She raised her glass and clinked it against his. "I agree. Here's to having fun together."

## 10

CAREN FOUND SHE enjoyed posing for Tate. Although they seldom talked during her modeling sessions, there was a feeling of warm intimacy in just being together. Her limbs did ache after an hour or so of maintaining a single position, but she was never bored; she had a rare opportunity to watch her husband absorbed in the creative process, and she never tired of studying his handsome, mobile features.

She was disappointed, however, that Tate refused to let her see any of his sketches of her.

"I'd rather you didn't look at the work in progress," he said. "When the whole series is finished, we'll have an unveiling. But until then, promise me you won't be tempted to peek when I'm not around."

"I can't promise not to be tempted," she said ruefully, "but I will promise to resist the temptation."

The upcoming Cross-Country Ski Club social offered another opportunity for togetherness. They
shopped together for new, matching black ski outfits,
and though Tate took full responsibility for waxing
the skis and getting them in order, the making of their
culinary contribution for the event was a joint effort.
They decided to bring cabbage rolls, and under Tate's
supervision, Caren prepared the filling, while Tate
actually stuffed the rolls and made the sauce.

Luckily, there was a fresh fall of snow overnight.
Caren and Tate hadn't skied since the previous winter,
so they were both a little rusty, and it wasn't long
before the rest of the ski club was well ahead of them.

"It's a good thing it's a short course," Caren said,
huffing and puffing behind Tate, who seemed to be
picking up speed.

He looked over his shoulder. "If you want to stop,
just give a shout. I don't want you to overdo it."

Caren shouted back, "I'm fine," but she was becoming uncomfortably aware of how out of shape she
really was. Tate was skiing easily now; he had the
type of lean build that was just made for athletics.
But Caren found the exercise fatiguing, and after a
while she had to stop.

She called out to Tate, and sank awkwardly into
the snow.

He came skiing back to her at a furious pace and
hurled himself down beside her. When he was sure
she wasn't injured, he smiled and stuck out his hand
to help her up. "Come on, lazybones," he teased.
"This is no place to take a rest."

"It's okay for you to laugh," she told him, un-
wanted tears filling her eyes. *"You* didn't have half

a baby last year." The minute she'd said the words she regretted them, but if he thought her accusation unfair, Tate gave no sign.

His hand slipped to her waist. "Does it hurt anywhere?"

"Only inside my head." She leaned her forehead against his cold, nylon-clad arm. "What's wrong with me, Tate?"

He tugged her woolen cap down over her ears. "I don't think it's anything to do with the baby. I'm tired, too. We're out of shape because we haven't done much this winter."

"I suppose you're right," she agreed.

He smiled. "For once I think I am. Caren you're fine. You're just growing. Already you're using some of your energy to create works of art. I know it hurts, but as an artist I've learned how to use that pain constructively. I ached to have my work appreciated by my peers, and then when I had that I ached for something else." He stroked her wind-flushed cheek. "I was lonely. Not because I was alone—I don't mind that aspect—but inside my head. I needed someone really close to understand me. You fulfill that need. Having a child would be great, but I'll always need you first and foremost."

Caren sniffed. "Quite some speech, Ashley."

He quirked a dark eyebrow. "A speech I might not have been capable of making six months ago."

"Then you've grown, too?"

"Seems that way," he said softly, offering her his hand. "Come on, I'll go slower so you can keep up."

With Tate striding alongside her at a much slower pace, Caren managed to finish the entire course. They met the other members of the club outside the town hall where they were to have the buffet and dance.

"How nice to see you both." Grace Stark smiled, and her husband, Ray, echoed her greeting. "Come on inside. They're serving hot chocolate while we get the food out on the tables. Your cabbage rolls look delicious, Caren."

"Tate shares the blame for them," Caren said, feeling better. She had been a little apprehensive about attending this affair, almost like a child taking its first few tentative steps, but now she was glad she'd come.

"How nice to have a man who cooks," Grace said with a pointed look at her husband.

"I do everything else," Ray Stark complained, and with a burst of laughter the four entered the hall.

A banner strung across one end of the room announced that this was the Russelton Cross-Country Ski Club Buffet and Dance, and a disc jockey was setting up piles of 45's on a table covered with purple velvet; otherwise, the hall's pale green walls and wooden floors were unadorned.

Caren and Tate joined a group of friends, most of them Caren's customers, and stood there talking about the skiing, the weather, and the food that was to come. Caren was rather surprised to see David walk in the door. He was with a dark-haired woman, and they were both wearing jeans and blue cotton shirts.

David spotted Caren and Tate and came straight over to them.

"Hi." Caren smiled. "I didn't know you were coming."

"I missed the skiing because I had to drive down to London to pick up Judy." He drew the hazel-eyed girl toward Caren and Tate. "This is Judy Steen. Judy, this is Caren and Tate Ashley."

Judy smiled and held out a slim hand. "I'm really pleased to meet you both. David's told me so much about you." She shook hands with Caren, and then turned to Tate, who was appraising the brunette in much the same way Caren was. David usually went for very glamorous women, and although Judy was pretty with her long, silky, deep brown hair and nice white smile, she certainly wasn't David's usual type.

"Good to meet you," Tate said thoughtfully, while Caren gave him a poke in the thigh that meant, Behave in front of David. "Hi, David."

"Hi, Tate. It's good to see you both out."

"We thought we'd better get the most out of our dues," said Caren, "seeing as we paid for two years in a row."

"That's my partner, as mercenary as ever," David joked. He took hold of Judy's hand in a companionable manner, and said, "Well, we're going to get some of that delicious-looking food. What did you bring, Caren?"

"Tate and I made the cabbage rolls at the far end," she told him.

"Lucky lady, your husband helps with the cooking," Judy said. "We'll go try them out first. I love cabbage rolls."

As the two walked away, Caren glanced at Tate. "Do I smell romance in the air?"

"Certainly not his usual glitzy type," Tate remarked. "Has he said anything?"

"Now that you mention it, he has," Caren told him. "He told me that he'd found someone who liked to make love in the morning."

Tate eyed Judy's departing shapely form. "Really, I hope he is serious. It'll get him off your back."

"He's never been on..." Caren's voice trailed off as she realized he was teasing. "Anyhow, you were very polite to him tonight."

"It's the first time I've seen him that I haven't wanted to put my fist through his face," Tate said.

"You're so violent, Ashley, but I love your jealousy. Come on, let's get some of that food before it's all gone."

"You're feeling better now, I take it?" Tate asked as they sauntered to the table to pick up paper plates and cutlery.

"Much better. I think you were right. I do need to get out among people and do things. I've been living too much inside my head."

"I keep telling you I'm right," he teased, pushing her ahead of him. "Save something for me on your way through."

After dinner, draft beer and soft drinks were served to accompany the top-forty hits that were being played. Card tables were set around the hall, and David and Judy shared one with Tate and Caren. In the course of their conversation, it came out that Judy was a potter, too.

"Oh no, not another one," Tate groaned. "I'm surrounded."

But Caren noticed how relaxed he seemed with David, and that was a plus for both of them. For years she had been hoping that the two men would become friends.

The music was pounding loudly, and Caren was tapping her toe on the floor.

"Want to dance?" Tate asked.

"Do you?"

"Would I ask if I didn't?"

"I guess not," she said gaily, allowing herself to be dragged onto the dance floor.

Caren had such a wonderful time that she was sorry when it was all over. She leaned her head on Tate's shoulder as they drove home in the van.

"Someone's sleepy," he remarked.

She fluttered her eyelashes. "I'm exhausted."

"Then you might not have the energy for my night-cap," he said.

"Depends on what it is," she said, chuckling.

At home they made love with abandon, then fell fast asleep in the tangle of sheets.

Caren stood speechless before the six canvases that constituted *Portraits of My Love*. They were certainly the best work Tate had ever done, but that didn't account for the huge lump in her throat. Despite the difficult period they'd been through, these paintings once and for all resolved any doubts Caren had of her husband's love. For the first time, she saw herself through his eyes: a vision of loveliness surrounded by an enchanted aura at the lake; a seductive odalisque stretched out before the hearth; a fairy-tale bride; and even, in the portrait of her in the kitchen stirring the first pot of soup she had ever made, a personification of the Victorian angel in the house. Caren smiled to herself. Little would the viewer guess that the artist had stood behind the model giving her detailed instructions for every step in the preparation of that soup!

But it was the final two portraits that moved her so inexplicably. She'd had reservations about posing in the nude for the fifth painting, even though Tate had assured her the picture wouldn't be too revealing. He'd shown her in their bed, a sheet draped discreetly over the lower half of her body, and her torso in profile, but it was clearly a portrait of a woman who'd just been made love to. It showed Caren exactly the way she felt after she and Tate made love—radiant, fulfilled, awed by the mystery of their intimacy. The woman of this painting was different from the others—less ethereal, the angel made woman and lover. It was a powerful painting, but the final portrait of the series—the one Caren hadn't knowingly posed for—was even more powerful. It showed her at the shop, the day Tate had come in to find her staring at the rough model of the boy's head that her fingers had seemed to shape of their own will. Tate had caught her surprise, and so many other emotions she hadn't been aware of—wistfulness, tenderness, and a sense of resolution, too, as if the figure marked some kind of turning point in her feelings about the lost baby.

As perhaps it had, Caren realized, for even her brief outburst on the ski slopes hadn't been about the child so much as about herself. Since losing the baby she'd had a feeling of discontent and incompleteness, but that was separate from the sorrow and grief for the child who would never be. In creating the bust, she had somehow laid to rest those feelings of intense loss and mourning, and Tate must have sensed that, for his portrait conveyed the healing process even as it was taking place.

"Caren?" Tate murmured against her ear. "You haven't said a word. You don't like them? Is it just that you feel they're too personal, or do you really think they're bad?"

"Bad! Tate, they're extraordinary!" she cried, turning to face him. "I didn't say anything because I was too overcome for speech. But they're masterpieces, every one of them."

"You really think so?" he said eagerly. "I felt I had surpassed myself, but I was afraid that might just be because I'm so in love with the subject."

"The paintings show how much," she said with a tremulous smile. "Sometimes I think you understand my feelings better than I understand them myself. But the subjective aspect apart, they're magnificent works of art—the colors, the composition...This series will establish you as a major artist, Tate, I'm sure of it. Even your father will have to acknowledge your work then."

The words had just slipped out, but she wasn't sorry. Tate had painted eleven important works recently, and their relationship was deepening day by day; this seemed as good a time as any to broach the subject of his father.

But the bitterness of his laughter made her uneasy. "Let's not mar a beautiful moment by talking about my father, all right, Caren?"

"Tate, when I stayed at your parents' house, your mother and I talked about your relationship with your father and—"

"She had no right to say anything!" he burst out fiercely. "I've tried to keep him out of anything to do with us, Caren. In fact, I wish I could keep him out of my life altogether."

She put a hand on his arm. "I know, Tate, but I don't think that's right. You've shared my pain, darling, and I want to share yours."

"I got over that pain a long time ago."

"No, you just shelved it."

His face darkened. "Caren, I don't want to talk about it."

She sighed. If she pushed the issue, it might lead to another estrangement between them, and she didn't want that. But she felt that unless Tate finally resolved the painful feelings about his father, there would always be a shadow over their love.

The gallery opening was only three weeks away. Tate had spent most of the last week down in London, getting preparations under way for the show. It was all complete except for a final painting, an abstract study in color, and that was close to being finished. Tate had wanted an even dozen pictures for the exhibition, although Tanya had only asked for eight.

Caren made the most of the time with Tate away to clean the house and shop. She felt lonely without him, missed him terribly. They had become so close lately, making love so regularly, that she felt his absence even more intensely. We have to be away from each other sometimes, she told herself sternly, throwing her excess energy into her work.

But one day as she was wandering around his studio, studying his work, she felt such love that she wondered what she would do if she ever lost him. Then she began to worry about his driving home that night in the freezing rain that was falling. She got herself into such a panic that she phoned his mother's house to see if he'd left yet.

"An hour or so ago," Donna said. "I wouldn't worry. Tate's a careful driver."

"I'm thinking of crazier drivers than Tate," Caren said ruefully. She hung up feeling isolated. At times like this she wished she had a television set. She turned on the radio for what little company it offered, and made a pot of herbal tea. She was just about to pour herself a cup when the garage door banged open.

She hardly gave Tate a chance to get through the door, before she hurled herself into his arms.

"That's the kind of welcome, I like," he said, giving her a big hug.

"I was so worried."

"Why?"

"The freezing rain, and I've missed you, darling."

"The roads were only wet, not icy, and I've missed you, too, but the show's finally set."

"Come have some tea and tell me all about it." She dragged him by the hand. Suddenly, the house was alive again.

"I'm going to take the paintings down next week," Tate told Caren. "Want to come along for the ride? I thought we'd stay a day or so with Mom and Dad."

"I'm certainly not staying here alone," Caren said. "I need to be with you."

The following Friday they carefully packed the paintings in the back of the van between cardboard and plastic. Tate was insisting that Caren take her wall hanging with the shell motif to show Tanya and Ben. He had a feeling they might be able to sell it. Caren really didn't like to horn in on his success, but he insisted.

"Look what you've done for me," he said. "I've finished more paintings in one stretch than ever before. I'm having a show that I think will be interesting and hopefully successful. And that hanging is great. You've said you no longer find the shop so challenging; this could open up a whole new area for you."

"Okay." She shrugged. "We'll show them."

"You bet we will."

It was a happy trip down to London. The snow was melting in the city and the grass was turning green. They delivered the paintings to the back of the gallery. Ben and Tate carried them in while Caren and Tanya supervised.

"You two are a lot of help," Ben said. "Why don't you go make us coffee?"

"Okay," Tanya told him, and the two women went upstairs to the apartment.

Caren loved Tanya and Ben's apartment. It was unusually wide open and spacious. All the plants, labeled because they were so unusual, were in huge white pots.

Scrutinizing Tanya in her black smock and jeans, Caren said, "You're not showing yet." She was pleasantly surprised to see how easily she could speak of the other woman's pregancy.

Tanya was fixing coffee in a white ceramic coffeemaker. "You don't think so?"

Caren narrowed her eyes, relieved to find that she now felt nothing but pleasure for Tanya. "Well, maybe you do look a bit larger around the chest. And I guess your tummy's filling out."

"Ben thinks I look gorgeous, but I'm feeling like a ten-ton weight."

"Wait until you're about eight months along," Caren said.

"I'll be like a lead balloon. Ben'll have to carry me down the stairs. You don't think we're crazy having babies at our age, do you?"

"All you need is love—and you two have plenty of that," Caren said. "Don't worry, Tanya."

Tanya nodded in agreement. "Our relationship is

really good. We haven't had a problem for years now.
At first it was so up and down. Sometimes I thought
the marriage wouldn't last."

"I never knew that." Caren had always thought
Tanya and Ben the best of friends and lovers.

"Well, we never told the world. You know how it
is . . . you like people to think you're making a success
of everything. We always had passionate loving,
though. I think that made us stick."

"It's like that with Tate," Caren admitted. "The
loving is so good."

"His pictures of you speak volumes about that.
Listen, Caren, it's nice to have a baby, just as an
added bonus, but your man's the most important thing."

"I know," Caren agreed. "Although I think I forgot
it for a while."

Tanya put the coffee and cups on a tray, and Caren
took if from her. "I'll carry this," she said. "I don't
want you falling down the stairs."

They spent the rest of the morning and half the
afternoon unpacking Tate's work and storing it in the
back room in preparation for hanging. Tate brought
forward Caren's wall hanging, much to her embarrassment. She had never considered herself an artist.

"It's great," Tanya enthused. "Why don't you do
some more and we'll put you in our crafts show next
fall? You can have a corner dedicated to Caren Bryant
Ashley."

"Tanya, it's not that good," Caren protested.

"Put her down for the show," Tate said. "She's
already done another hanging, and I'll crack the whip
till she's got four or five. I'll also select some of her
pottery pieces to go with them."

"Tate!" Caren objected.

He gave her long hair a gentle tug. "Don't be such a spoilsport. What's wrong with trying to establish a name for yourself? You can do it, too. I know you can."

"But I'm just a small-town potter. I'm no artist."

"But this is good," Ben said softly. "You're developing, Caren. Let it flow. None of us would say you were good if we didn't mean it. We're your friends, but we're honest about art."

"Russelton will be too small to handle you soon." Tate picked her up to swing her around the gallery.

"Next you'll be having me painting masterpieces," Caren complained. "Tate's the artist."

"Then how come the mugs I have in this house are the best pottery I've seen for a long time?" Tanya interjected.

"Because I'm a potter. That's my craft. My shop is my work."

"Where's your spirit of adventure?" Tate asked, still holding her around the waist. "We'll take the world by storm—the artistic Ashleys."

Caren laughed. "Okay, I'll do some more, but I'm not guaranteeing anything."

"As long as you guarantee me at least three hangings plus this one, and Tate sorts out the pots," Tanya told her. "Now scram, you two. Didn't I hear Tate say something about buying you a dress for the opening, Caren?"

Tate hadn't said anything about a dress, but he took the hint and drove the van to a small but expensive boutique where Caren had shopped once before.

Inside they went through the rack until together they spotted a calf-length green silk dress. Tate pulled the dress off the rack. "What do you think?"

Caren checked the price tag and winced. "Don't look at that." She ran her fingers over the soft material. "It's real silk, isn't it?"

"If you like it, I'm going to buy it for you, Caren," Tate said. "You deserve it. Go try it on."

It looked gorgeous on her. The supple silk fell easily over her hips, emphasizing her long, shapely legs. The sleeves flowed to her wrists, and the neckline was a low V that accented her creamy cleavage. The color reflected her eyes. She drew her hair on top of her head and posed. "What do you think?"

"It's you," he said with certainty and turned to the sales clerk. "We'll take it."

"Do you need new shoes for this?" Tate asked when they were back in the van.

"My black suede sandals will be perfect," Caren said. "The dress is beautiful, darling. What are you wearing for the opening?"

"I'll wear my black velvet suit," he said.

"With underwear, I hope."

"With underwear," he confirmed, remembering their three-and-a-half-year anniversary celebration.

## — 11 —

TATE'S MOTHER WAS home when they arrived at the senior Ashleys' house. Dressed in a black wool sheath and slim high heels, Donna was waiting on the step for them. "How good to see you both together," she said, hugging them close.

"Are you getting excited, Tate?"

"It's pretty thrilling." He smiled affectionately at his mother. "We're planning on staying a couple of nights this time, by the way."

"Good, because I've already invited the boys over for Saturday dinner. We're all coming to the opening next week."

"And Dad?" Tate asked as they went in through the front door.

"Well..." Donna sighed. "Maybe we can talk him

into it. If George walks into an art gallery, then he will be retracting everything he has always said. Let's see if he can be humble."

Tate shrugged, still carrying their bags, but Caren knew his father's attitude still hurt him. "Are we in the rose room upstairs?" he asked his mother.

"Of course. Go and get settled and I'll bring some tea in to the back room. George won't be home for a couple of hours, and we can have a chat."

Up in the guest room, Caren touched Tate's arm. "Don't let your dad bother you," she said softly. "Don't let him spoil this for you."

"I won't," he said, shrugging off her hand to walk into the bathroom. He closed the door and Caren raised her eyes to the flowered ceiling. If only Tate would face his pain and deal with it.

Caren straightened her yellow silk blouse and smoothed her jeans and hair. She unpacked the dress she had brought along for the following evening's dinner and sat on the edge of the bed to wait for Tate.

When he came out of the bathroom, he'd combed his hair and he smelled of soap. He squatted by her legs. "Look, Caren, there's nothing you can do about my dad and me. It's a never-ending saga, like a damn soap opera. I've accepted it."

"I don't believe that," she told him. "I think it bothers you no end."

"Okay, it bothers me, but what the hell can I do?"

"Accept him."

"I do accept him. But he can't accept me. That's the contention in this war." He stood up and stuffed his hands into the back pockets of his tight jeans. "Oh, for heaven's sake, Caren; let's not fight about it. My father shouldn't come between you and me."

Caren stood up. "What affects you, affects me. I feel hurt for you, Tate."

He stared down at her and then kissed her nose. "I don't want you bothered with this."

"Well I *am* bothered, and you can't do much about it." She shrugged. "Come on, we'd better go down and join your mom."

Hand in hand, they walked down the carpeted staircase and into the living room. Donna was sitting on the sofa pouring tea into delicate china cups. There was a grand array of goodies on a plate: slices of banana loaf, homemade strawberry tarts, brownies.

Tate popped a whole tart into his mouth. "This is delicious."

"I made them this morning." Donna smiled at her son. "Sit down, you two. Tell me everything you've been doing."

For the next two hours, they talked nonstop, covering everything from Tate's work to Caren's new culinary efforts to Tanya's pregnancy. Then, suddenly, the front door banged.

"That's George." Donna straightened on the couch. She glanced at Tate. "Take it easy."

"I'm loose," he said.

Donna went to greet her husband. When George walked into the room, Caren felt Tate tense beside her. Then he stood up and said, "Hi, Dad."

"Son, how are you? It's good to see you. Caren, you look lovely."

Caren stood up while they all shook hands formally.

Donna patted her husband's arm. "Why don't you go up and change out of that suit, George? Then we'll have dinner. I know you like to eat right away."

"I sure do. It's hard work running that company."
He smiled at everyone. "I won't be long. Donna, how
about some drinks for everyone?"

"All right," she said. But when George had left,
she glanced at Tate and Caren. "Do you really want
a drink?"

"Not particularly," Tate said. "I've hardly touched
hard liquor in years."

"Good. I'll just go check on dinner. You should
take a walk in the backyard, now that the snow's gone.
The crocuses and tulips are lovely."

When they were alone, Tate opened the French
windows and they walked out on to the paved pathway. The entire place smelled of earth and growing
things. Purple and white crocuses lined the path, and
red tulips bloomed along the warm brick wall of the
house. Tate took Caren's hand and they wandered in
silence, walking beneath the trellises that in summer
would be laden with roses. Tate stopped to kiss her
behind the little gazebo.

Caren dreamily wound her arms around her husband's neck and returned the kiss warmly. They both
tasted of the outdoors and spring. Arms around each
other, they returned to the house.

Caren admired the way Donna engineered the conversation at dinner. Not a mention was made of the
construction industry or art. Both subjects were deftly
avoided while Donna talked about her volunteer work
and the Ashleys' plans for retirement in Florida, then
mentioned some friends that Tate had known, which
drew him into the conversation. The entire meal went
smoothly.

The rest of the evening was spent lounging on the
soft, well-worn leather furniture in the comfortable

family room. The large color television was turned
on, and they all sat and watched a movie. Since Caren
and Tate didn't own a TV set, it was always a treat
to see a good show.

Finally, in bed in the rose room, they lay nestled
together, chatting about the day. Tate explained how
he wanted his show set up in the gallery, although he
knew Tanya and Ben would have their very vocal say
in the matter.

"It's their gallery, Tate," Caren said. "You have
to compromise."

"I know." He sighed, his mind distracted, as he
ran his hand over her shapely thighs.

She parted her legs and let him touch her, and then
rolled over and kissed his arm. "Want something?"

"It must be the color of this room, but I always
get so turned on here." He grinned and drew her
fingers over to his body. "Feel that."

"Mr. Ashley!" she exclaimed, thrilling to the touch
of his male hardness.

"Shush, they'll hear us," he whispered, but Caren
was already in his arms.

They lay face to face, kissing, stroking. Tate's
expert caresses ignited white-hot desire everywhere
he touched, and Caren could gauge his own passion
by his ragged breathing. Excitement boiled out of
control and they moved together in a frenzy, trying
to keep silent. But Caren couldn't help crying out her
pleasure, it was more than she could bear.

After breakfast on Saturday morning, George
seemed intent on monopolizing Tate's attention. Donna
had gone out to the supermarket, so Caren followed
the two men around the house as George proudly

showed off the improvements he'd made since Christmas—a new bathroom, workshop, and tool-storage space built in the basement.

"What do you think, Tate?" George asked, waving one hand at his collection of tools.

"It looks great to me, Dad," Tate said. "Something you can really use when you retire."

"That's what I thought," George replied, leading the way into the workshop. He walked to one corner and pulled out a cardboard box. "While I was cleaning up, I found some of your stuff." He pulled at a couple of sheets of masonite that Caren saw had paintings on one side. "You might as well take this junk home, Tate."

*Junk!* George Ashley was actually calling Tate's work *junk!* Caren almost hurled herself at him, but stepped back into the shadows, loath to interfere. She watched Tate's face tighten and his lips grow white as he tried to control himself.

Caren expected an outburst, but Tate just shrugged. "Sure, why not." She had a feeling that they were the only words he could get out.

Tate leaned over and opened one side of the box. He pulled out a couple of brushes and a congealed paint pot. He tossed them back into the box and glanced around the workshop. "This place is great, Dad. Now I have some things to do."

Tate brushed passed Caren and took the carpeted stairs two at a time. After a few seconds, she heard the front door crash.

George Ashley glanced at Caren. "What's with him?"

"I think I'll find out," she said tersely, and turned

abruptly, leaving George Ashley alone. As she went upstairs, she felt like screaming.

Caren knew that Tate was probably out at the gazebo, but she didn't try to follow him. He needed to be alone for a while. When Donna arrived home, her arms full of groceries, Caren was in the kitchen making coffee and George Ashley was down in his workshop with a power drill going.

"What a racket," Donna closed the kitchen door. "Where's Tate?"

"He's gone out for a while," Caren said, leaning against the counter.

Donna raised a dark eyebrow. "Did he have a fight with his dad?"

"Not a fight exactly," Caren clarified. "George had found some of Tate's stuff in the basement, and referred to it as 'junk.'"

"Leave those two alone for five minutes and there are bound to be fireworks. You know what it is, Caren? George feels that if he pressures Tate about the worthlessness of his art, then Tate will eventually come around to his way of thinking and join the business."

Caren sighed. "Why doesn't he just give up?"

Donna put butter and bacon into the fridge. "I don't know how many times I've said those very words. Pride's a pretty heavy thing to move aside."

"I know," Caren said. She heard the door slam and Tate's footsteps on the stairs. She filled a mug with coffee and went to the bedroom.

Tate was sprawled on the bed, his arms beneath his head.

Caren put her mug on the night table and sat down beside him.

"Why don't you fight back, Tate?"

"He's my father, Caren," he said harshly. "Anyway, let's not talk about it."

Caren respected Tate's wishes and left him alone. When she returned to the bedroom in midafternoon to change into her black wool shirtwaist and high heels before Harry and Ron arrived with their families, Tate was sitting on the bed with his knees drawn up, reading a book.

"You'll have to come down sometime," she said, as she brushed her hair.

Tate tossed his paperback carelessly on to the floor, and slipped his legs over the side of the bed. "I'm right with you."

The house seemed to erupt as soon as Tate's brothers and their families arrived. Harry and Ron were both huge men who took after George. Mary was dark and petite, always worrying about her five-year-old son, Mark, and patting the head of her twelve-year-old daughter, Shelley. Ron and Laura only had one child. Her name was Jean and she was sixteen, with brown curly hair like her mother's. She was at the sulky age where all she wanted to do was listen to rock music and not talk to adults. Tate hadn't seen her for a while, but he was the only one who could talk to her. Caren suspected it was because Tate treated Jean like an adult and not a child.

Caren always enjoyed these family get-togethers even with the obvious undercurrents. Being the only child of rather reserved parents, she had never experienced the kind of give and take, laughter, and arguing that were characteristic of mealtimes at the Ashley home. Nor had she ever had to fight for her parents' love or attention. She'd been the darling of their lives, the little girl they'd always wanted. Tate, on the other hand, had two very large brothers, confident of their place in the community and in their father's good graces.

With his whole family around him, George was more domineering than ever, and this time even Donna's calming influence and carefully engineered speech patterns had little effect on him. He drank too much scotch and went on and on about his work.

At dinner, which was roast beef with all the trimmings, he coached Harry on how it would be when he ran the company, and Ron on how he would need to support Harry. The boys just looked bland; they'd obviously heard it all before. George even jumped on young Mark, telling him that he would one day be in the business.

Jean looked bored with the entire affair and sighed as if the world really didn't have a place for her. Had Tate felt this way at one time? Caren wondered. Tate was certainly the odd one out, except for his mother.

It was Laura who brought him into the conversation. "We're all coming to the opening of your show," she told Tate. "We're so proud of you."

"Pansy stuff," George snorted. "You won't get me there."

There was a long silence during which everyone looked uncomfortable.

"Come on, Dad," Harry said. "You'll enjoy it."

George banged his fist on the table, his inhibitions lowered by all the alcohol he'd consumed. "I've said I'll never go into one of those places. I know you young people think it's trendy and all that; but as far as I'm concerned, it's a waste of time."

"George!" Donna looked as if she wanted to say

more but didn't want to cause Tate further embarrassment.

The muscles in Tate's jaw tightened, and his face was chalk white. Take it, he told himself. You've taken it for thirty-three years.

Watching her husband suppress his anger and hurt, Caren felt her own fury at George Ashley boil over. "How dare you!" she flung at Tate's father. "Tate's your son. You should be proud of him. He's an extremely sensitive and talented artist. He's brilliant at his work. Not everyone is cut out for mucking around on a construction site, or working in an office nine to five. I'm not, for one, and neither is Tate. He wanted to be something in the world, more than just one of the workers. I'm not underrating what you do, but some of us have a different mission. I love Tate very much, and I'm extremely proud of his work. He's a great husband, a talented painter, and one of the best men in the world." She broke down then, tears streaming down her face. "Please..." She ran blindly from the dining room and stumbled up the stairs.

In the bedroom, she stood holding herself tight. What the hell had she done? She would never be able to face Tate's father again, and maybe not even his brothers. Donna might understand, but Caren knew she had been extremely rude to George.

The door opened, and she turned to see Tate through a mist of tears.

"Caren, darling." He gathered her into his arms. "I was touched by everything you said, but you didn't have to defend me to him. It doesn't matter."

"It does matter," Caren said. "It does matter, Tate. It matters to me an awful lot. He shouldn't be allowed to get away with remarks like that."

"I know, I know. Just forget it."

"How can I forget it?" she sobbed. "How can I face them all again?"

"You can face them. He deserved it. Even Ron and Harry will admit that. Now come on down. Don't leave it so long that there will be permanent damage. We haven't had dessert yet."

He waited while she washed her face and repaired her makeup and then led her into the dining room. This time he sat close beside her, his hard thigh comforting against hers.

"I'm sorry," Caren said, glancing warily at them all, especially George.

"It's okay," Donna said softly, smiling at her. "It's been coming for a long time. George do you want dessert?"

"Yes," he said abruptly.

The rest of the dinner was rather subdued. The evening picked up a little when Jean put some of her new albums on the stereo and Harry and Ron recounted some hilarious tales of last year's vacation to the Caribbean.

But when they all finally left, Caren felt drained and ill. A headache was throbbing loudly in her temples.

"I'd like to go home tonight," she told Tate.

"Okay, we will. Go pack up the stuff. I'll talk to Mom."

They said a strained good-bye to Tate's father, but Donna saw them out to the van.

"Don't feel bad," she told Caren, giving her a hug. "I'll talk to him. I'm still going to try and get him to the opening. I think it's time for someone to pave the

way for peace. There's enough hostility in the world
without having it fester within your own family."

"You can't force him," Caren said with a sigh.

"He loves Tate, whatever you might think. Maybe
I can convince him to do it for that reason."

Tate jumped down from the van where he'd packed
the luggage. "Bye, Mom."

"Bye, dear." Donna and Tate hugged. "Don't take
it too hard."

"I'm used to it," he said, but when they were on
their way up to Russelton, Caren saw his expression
alter as if his thoughts weren't pleasant.

By the time they reached home, Tate wasn't in a
very good mood at all. Caren took a hot bath and an
aspirin and got ready for bed. She felt very tense, and
her head wouldn't stop pounding. She'd never done
anything like that in her life before. Of course, she'd
never been married to Tate before. Nothing had ever
meant this much to her.

She was sitting on the bed in her green nightgown,
brushing her hair, when Tate popped his head into the
room. "I've made some cocoa if you want to talk."

"I'll be right down," she told him.

They sat in the kitchen, opposite each other, drink-
ing the cocoa.

"I hate him," Tate said after a while. "I hate him
for drawing you into this stupid argument."

"You don't hate him," Caren said. "Why don't you
talk to him?"

"I've tried. It's like talking to a brick wall. He
won't give an inch."

"Leave it, Tate." She was completely exhausted.
She wanted to ask him other questions, but she de-

cided to wait until after the opening. She didn't want him any more upset than he already was.

The unpleasant scene with George left Caren feeling heavyhearted. She knew she would have to snap out of it, though. The gallery opening was looming, and Tate was busy preparing for it. Both of them seemed to be forcing the gaiety somewhat, and Caren felt sick about that. If only George would come to the opening. Why couldn't he relent? She considered phoning him and begging, but then thought better of it. What could she say? The man had a closed mind.

She did phone Tate's sisters-in-law, however. Laura and Mary assured her that they'd both be attending the opening with their husbands.

"I'm proud to have a famous brother-in-law," Mary told her. "And I'm so glad you stood up to George. I've always wanted to say something like that myself, but I never had the guts."

"It was probably a bit rude in his own house," Caren said.

"Well, I think he deserved it. That's a sick thing to say to Tate. I'll tell you, Harry doesn't agree with his father either. He just hasn't had a reason to fight him like Tate. Ron and Harry admire Tate."

"I'm glad," Caren said, relieved to learn this. She had always thought that Harry and Ron were completely on George's side.

"Anyhow," Mary went on, "I just want you to know that the rest of us are looking forward to the opening."

"Thanks, Mary," Caren said gratefully. "We'll see you there, then."

"Bye, Caren. Don't worry."

The day of the opening dawned sunny and warm. Caren had taken the day off from work, and she went for a walk by the lake in the morning. The blue water was dotted with whitecaps, and the sky was a deeper blue with little white fluffy clouds. She hoped the lovely day was a good omen for the coming evening.

She bathed early and slipped into her new green dress. Then she twisted her hair on top of her head and fastened a gold locket around her neck; it was something Tate had given her when they married. She topped it all off with a dressy light-weight black coat. With matching black shoes and small suede purse on a chain-link handle, she decided the effect was feminine yet sophisticated. She wanted to look her best for Tate's sake.

"Good enough to eat," he told her as he straightened a black silk tie over his white shirt. He shrugged on the black velvet jacket that matched his pants. "How do I look?"

"Good enough to eat. Everyone will know you're the artist."

He grinned. "I always thought I should grow a beard and really act the part."

"You do and I'll vacate your bed." Caren leaned over to kiss his smoothly shaven cheek. "It would tickle."

"It might add a new dimension to our lovemaking."

Caren sighed dramatically. "I don't need any added dimensions. I'm exhausted from it already."

"Damn, I was going to make love to you before we left."

"Ho, ho," she laughed, and raced down the stairs before he could catch her.

They were taking David and Judy to the opening, and they drove downtown in Caren's car. They honked the horn outside David's apartment, and David and Judy came running out and scrambled into the back seat.

"Congratulations, Tate." Judy looked glamorous in a silky black pants suit beneath a short maroon poodle coat. "Are you nervous?"

"I'm full of butterflies," Tate admitted. "I always imagine the fully lit gallery, wine and cheese and coffee ready, and no one comes."

David laughed. "I've never been to an opening where no one came. Don't worry. You've been well publicized. We were down in London the other night and heard an announcement on the radio."

"Tanya's planning on getting her money's worth," Caren said. She managed a peep into the back and saw that David's arm was possessively around Judy's shoulders. Those two seemed a good match.

The talk was lively all the way into London as they sped along the highway. They had arranged to have dinner at a little French restaurant. David, who had insisted on making the meal his treat, held up his wineglass: "To a great couple, and also to Tate's show. We're with you, Tate."

"Thanks," Tate said, feeling a bit sheepish. He wondered how he could ever have been so jealous of his wife's partner. He reached for Caren's hand beneath the red tablecloth. They had come through a crisis and survived.

They arrived at the gallery half an hour before the opening, which was set for eight o'clock. Tanya greeted them at the door, then locked it behind them.

"The artist has arrived," she called up the stairs to

Ben, who rushed down dressed in a red silk shirt and gray trousers.

Tanya was wearing a bright orange silk dress that was full enough to hide her burgeoning stomach. Her hair was a mass of curls around her thin face.

"How are you feeling?" Caren asked.

"Wonderful. I only get sick in the mornings." Tanya made a face. "No, seriously, that's wearing off now, thank goodness."

They had a preview of the show. Caren thought everything looked fantastic. Her green eyes glowed with pleasure as she moved around the room with Judy and David.

"He's good," Judy said. "He makes me want to cry sometimes."

"Yes, he really is good," David agreed. "Those pictures of you are exceptional, Car."

"Aren't they!" she said proudly. She glanced at her watch and at Tate, who was sitting on the bottom step talking to Tanya. It was almost time to open the doors.

Caren found herself looking at her husband as if this were the first time she'd ever seen him. His hair was black and thick and well brushed, his face smoothly shaven, and his muscular figure looked trim in the black velvet suit. I love you, she thought. I love you so much.

He looked up at her and smiled softly, his blue eyes glistening with excitement.

"I love you," she mouthed.

"I love you," he mouthed back.

The doors opened. Tanya nervously ran around checking the coffee and wine temperature. She kept placing Tate in different positions as if he were a statue.

"I'll just lounge here," Tate said escaping her grasp at last. He leaned against the wall and made a face. "How's that?"

"Stand up straight, Tate Ashley," Tanya scolded, while Ben laughed indulgently.

"Leave him alone," Ben said at last. "Just relax, sweetheart."

"What if no one comes?" Tanya wailed.

"How many openings have we had?" Ben questioned.

"Hundreds."

"How many have been flops?"

"One or two."

"Unknown artists. We're dealing with a pro here. Come on, Tanya, snap out of it. Here's the first of the crowd."

By eight-thirty, it was hard to move in the little gallery space. Tate was kept occupied by his fans, who kept asking him to explain his work. Caren kept an eye on the door for his family. She saw Ron and Laura first, and then Mary and Harry, followed by Donna. Then she felt her breath catch in her throat. Walking through the door a couple of steps behind the rest of his family was George Ashley.

# 12

TATE WAS TRYING to explain the philosophy behind his paintings when his father walked into the gallery. He stopped in midsentence while the people he was talking to gazed around as if wondering what was wrong.

"You'll have to excuse me," he said, and wound his way through the crowds toward his family.

"I'm so pleased you all came," he said, shaking hands with his brothers and kissing his sisters-in-law and mother. He just looked at his father.

For a moment, there might not have been anyone else around them. Tate kept the expression on his face open and friendly. His father had done this for him. For George Ashley, this was as difficult a feat as climbing Mount Everest. Tate could only imagine what it must have cost him to swallow all his pride.

"Dad." Tate held out his hand. "I'm glad you came."

George touched his son's hand. "Caren convinced me I owed it to you. I guess I owe you an apology, too, son."

"Apology accepted."

Tate's eyes filled with tears. Not here, he thought, blinking them back. Why am I so damn sentimental? He caught Caren's green eyes looking at him with love and pride and he smiled at her. She'd done this whole thing. She'd fought to make their marriage work. She'd inspired him to paint enough for a show. She'd even gotten his father to take a giant step toward reconciliation. He was so damn proud of her. He ached with love.

"Well, come on in," he said huskily to his family. "There's wine and cheese and coffee and cake—lots of goodies, and of course my paintings. Let me know if you like them."

The women and his brothers filtered into the crowd, but his father remained beside him.

"Maybe you could show me around," George said. "Help me understand what it's all about."

"Of course. Why don't we start from the beginning," Tate said, leading his father over to *Breakaway*.

George bent to read the title card. "What's the little red dot for?" he asked.

"That means it's been purchased," Tate said.

"Somebody bought it?"

Tate smiled slightly. "A major gallery purchased it for their permanent collection."

George straightened and plunged his hands into the pockets of his gray pants. "It's good, son."

"Thanks. I realize this is a whole new world to you, Dad," Tate said. "I'd suggest you just let your mind wander freely and feel what you want."

George shook his head. "It's good craftsmanship and nice colors. I can't fault the design. You would have made a good draftsman, and you could have done some of my buildings."

"You're better at the buildings than I could ever be," Tate told him. "Let's both stick to our own talents, shall we?"

"You've always been a level above me, Tate."

Tate touched his father's arm for the first time that he could remember since he'd been a small child. "Not on a higher level—just a different one. The world needs all kinds of people, Dad."

"I guess so."

George seemed uncomfortable, so Tate dropped his hand. "You're more pratical than I am," he said. "I guess I'm just a bit of a dreamer."

"Like your mother," his father commented. "You were always like your mother."

Tate glanced over to where Donna was talking to Caren. "Nothing much wrong with her, is there?"

"No." George sighed. "There's nothing much wrong with Caren, either. I wouldn't have come here tonight if it hadn't been for her." He cleared his throat. "Anyhow, Tate, you've got a good woman there. Hang on to her."

"I intend to." Tate smiled, although his jaw ached and his throat felt choked. "Would you like to see the paintings I did of her?"

"I intend to see all your paintings," George said. "That's what I came for."

Tate shook his head in wonder. He'd never believed in miracles, but there was no other word for this.

Tate was high on exhilaration when the last person drifted away from the gallery long past ten o'clock, the official closing time. He glanced at Caren and noticed that she was flushed with excitement. She gave him the thumbs-up sign and he returned it.

"Come on upstairs," Tanya told them. "You, too, Judy and David."

It took a long time and many pots of herbal tea before they all calmed down. While the stereo played Mozart, the men shed their suit jackets and ties and the women their shoes. Naturally, the talk was all about the opening.

"That could only be called a success in capital letters," Tanya said. "All sold but one, and I'll probably buy that."

"You'll eat up all your profits." Tate laughed.

"A terrible businesswoman," Ben joined in, teasing. "Aren't you, my love?"

Tanya made a face at him. "You won't think so when we've taken our percentage from the sales tonight." She looked at Tate. "So how do you feel about your father coming?"

He shook his head. "Words fail me."

Tanya gave him an understanding look.

"He's softened at last, Tate. That's good. It's late, but it's good."

"I think so, too," Tate said.

They went on to discuss other things, and it was four in the morning when Tate and Caren dropped off a sleepy Judy and David at David's apartment. Then Tate drove down to the lakeshore and parked the car.

"Fancy a walk?" he asked.

"Sure." Caren nodded. "I don't think I'll be able to sleep tonight."

"I might not be able to sleep for a week." He smiled.

Caren slipped off her shoes and pantyhose in the car and Tate took off his boots and rolled up the cuffs of his pants. Hand in hand, they walked along the shore. The water, still icy from the long winter, chilled their toes, but the air was balmy and springlike. Morning spread a purple haze over everything.

"This is where we met," Caren mused.

"I turned around and saw a vision," Tate said. "I was in a foul mood that night—until I met you."

"I'm so glad you met me. I remember you seemed moody, and it interested me."

He sighed. "I'm not quite that moody now that you're in my life. I don't need to withdraw so much. I trust you with my thoughts."

She gave his hand a squeeze and then said tentatively, "You and your father seem to have made a new beginning tonight."

"I think so," Tate agreed. "I feel that at last he's gotten through to me, and I to him. We'll probably never fully understand each other—at least I don't believe he'll ever understand me—but we will be closer. I'm going to work on it."

"I'm so glad." She squeezed his hand again. "Tate, your mother told me about his challenging your manhood when you were seventeen."

There was a long silence and then Tate said quietly,

"Did she tell you his exact words?"

"No," Caren said softly. "Why don't you tell me, Tate?"

"He accused me of being a homosexual. I still can't understand how—or why—he came up with that theory, but he really got to me with it. I tried to put it out of my mind, but I couldn't. It was mainly that I wanted him to like me. But how can you disprove something like that? Even taking a wife isn't really proof. I loved the damn guy. I wanted him to think I was worthy of his name. I still do . . ." Tate's voice petered out into the night.

"So you thought the baby would prove it once and for all?" Caren said quietly as the wind washed around them.

"Yes." He nodded. "I thought the baby would do it. Isn't that how men prove they're men? They have lots of sons."

"I knew there was something," Caren said.

"I didn't want anything to happen to that baby. I wanted a boy especially. I never knew I would feel that way about a child. I had no idea until then how deep my father's influence went. It shouldn't have had anything to do with the situation, but I couldn't help it. I was obsessed with becoming a father. I didn't want to touch you or hurt you in case I did something to injure you or the baby."

"That's why you stopped making love to me before the miscarriage?"

"Yes." He sighed.

"I thought you didn't love me anymore because I wasn't a good cook, I was starting to look fat, or maybe you'd just grown tired of me. That's why I worked myself to the bone at the store. I wanted to blot out what was happening. Here I was, pregnant with your child, and you were moving farther and farther away from me. You hardly even smiled at me, or caressed me."

"If I touch you, I want you, Caren. I thought that if I kept my distance, then I wouldn't want you so much."

"I was so scared."

"Oh, angel." He turned and pulled her into his arms. "I'm sorry. It seems so stupid now. Why should I have to prove anything? I am who I am."

"You couldn't help it. What your father said was unforgivable." Caren wrapped her arms around his waist and hugged him. "But you should have told me, Tate. I would have understood."

"How could I tell you that?"

Caren leaned back in his arms. "You're more of a man than anyone I've ever known. Just because you don't dig ditches doesn't make you any less masculine."

"I know that, and you know that..."

"And, deep down, your dad knows it, too." Caren said. "He's just being defensive about your art, something he doesn't truly understand. Your brothers don't agree with him, neither does your mom, and I certainly don't."

Tate kissed her nose and traced his fingers around the gold heart-shaped locket at her slim throat. "What did I do to deserve you?"

"You love me." Her arms tightened. "Please love me, Tate."

"I do, I do," he moaned, bringing his mouth down to cover hers. She tasted sweet and her body was supple and warm in his arms. He lifted her slightly, and held her hard against him. This woman was his life.

Caren could tell from Tate's kiss that everything was healed again. Now there was no more restraint, no more holding back. His mouth devoured hers, his arms straining from the effort to control his passion. When his hands caressed her breasts, her own passion rose to meet his in urgent delight.

"Let's go home," Tate whispered, "and I'll show you just how much I love you."

Caren turned a radiant smile on him. "You may show me more than you think."

"What do you mean?"

"Don't you know what time of the month this is?" she asked, still smiling.

"Oh!" Tate said, understanding slowly dawning. "It's all right, Caren. We can take precautions."

"Absolutely not!" she said, laughing. "I've never felt more ready to have a baby, Tate."

"But the shop . . ."

"Don't worry about the shop. You know darn well I've been getting bored with it. And David's falling in love with a potter is providential. Earlier tonight I sounded Judy out about becoming part of Caren's Crafts. Well, she's totally enthusiastic about the idea. I think she'll do it, Tate. And that will give me plenty of time for other things."

"Like making wall hangings?"

"That, too. But primarily I'm talking about being a mother, Tate."

"You're sure, Caren?" he asked tenderly.

"I haven't got a reservation in the world."

He hugged her ecstatically. "Now I really can't wait to get home."

They grinned at each other, then turned back toward the car. As they walked, their arms around each other, Caren felt a great burst of contentment. It was almost as though her body was already vibrant with new life. Leaning back against the seat, she turned to Tate.

"Happy, darling?" he asked, smiling down into her glowing eyes.

"Yes," she said. And she was.

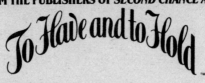

# DON'T MISS THESE TITLES
## IN THE
## SECOND CHANCE AT LOVE SERIES

### WINTER WILDFIRE #178
#### by Elissa Curry
Just who is tough guy Michael Moreno? A ruthless cad who's
at home in the underworld, or the compelling rogue
who delights in dishonoring his "gentleman's agreement"
with beautiful Chris Barnes?

### AFTER THE RAIN #179
#### by Aimée Duvall
Katrina is determined to triumph over Lockridge Advertising.
But her hopes are dashed when she's trapped in an elevator
with an oh, so witty, oh, so attractive stranger—
Mitchell Lockridge himself!

### RECKLESS DESIRE #180
#### by Nicola Andrews
Sandra Mandrell demands to be treated as a professional first and
a woman second . . . until she's thrown into competition with
Hank Donnell, whose amorous advances sabotage her good sense.

### THE RUSHING TIDE #181
#### by Laura Eaton
Divorced, with two teenagers, Julia Leighton can't afford dreams.
But Eric Spencer, a flamboyant oceanographer, sweeps her
to peaks of ecstasy and promises that wishes *can* come true . . .

### SWEET TRESPASS #182
#### by Diana Mars
Like an autumn bonfire, Barrett Shaw rages into Helena's world,
enflaming passions long forgotten, enveloping her
in a sensual haze. But her heart whispers urgent warnings . . .

### TORRID NIGHTS #183
#### by Beth Brookes
When Mackenna Scott's construction project in
lush Indonesia lags, her boss, Brock Hampton, dares to challenge
her ability . . . and overwhelm her senses.

#69

## HERE'S WHAT READERS
## ARE SAYING ABOUT

*To Have and to Hold*™

"Your TO HAVE AND TO HOLD series is
a fabulous and long overdue idea."
— *A. D., Upper Darby, PA\**

"I have been reading romance novels for over
ten years and feel the TO HAVE AND TO HOLD
series is the best I have read. It's exciting,
sensitive, refreshing, well written. Many thanks
for a series of books I can relate to."
— *O. K., Bensalem, PA\**

"I enjoy your books tremendously."
— *J. C., Houston, TX\**

"I love the books and read them over and over."
— *E. K., Warren, MI\**

"You have another winner with the new TO HAVE
AND TO HOLD series."
— *R. P., Lincoln Park, MI\**

"I love the new series TO HAVE AND TO HOLD."
— *M. L., Cleveland, OH\**

"I've never written a fan letter before, but
TO HAVE AND TO HOLD is fantastic."
— *E. S., Narberth, PA\**

\*Name and address available upon request